SUE HENRY

"Suspenseful, intelligent, and filled with the spectacular beauty of the northern wilds."

Chicago Sun-Times

"Chilling adventure . . . Henry has won well-deserved praise for the way she brings the history, lore, and beauty of an expansive wilderness to her heart-pounding plots."

Green Bay Press-Gazette

"[Henry's] descriptions of Alaska's wilderness make you want to take the next flight out, buy heavy sweaters, or at least curl up with an afghan, a cup of steaming hot chocolate, and the book."

Phoenix Gazette

"Twice as vivid as Michener's natural Alaska, at about a thousandth the length."

Washington Post Book World

"[Henry] has a way with Alaska's landscape, lore, and people."

Seattle Post-Intelligencer

"[Her] grasp of tense storytelling and strong characterization matches her with Sue Grafton. Give her a try—she'll challenge your powers of perception and deduction."

Colorado Springs Gazette Telegraph

Books by Sue Henry

DEATH TRAP
COLD COMPANY
DEAD NORTH
BENEATH THE ASHES
MURDER ON THE YUKON QUEST
DEADFALL
DEATH TAKES PASSAGE
SLEEPING LADY
TERMINATION DUST
MURDER ON THE IDITAROD TRAIL

SUE HENRY

DEATH TRAP

AN ALASKA MYSTERY

AVON BOOKS
An Imprint of Harper Collins*Publishers*

This is a work of fiction. Names, characters, places, and incidents are products of the author's imagination or are used fictitiously and are not to be construed as real. Any resemblance to actual events, locales, organizations, or persons, living or dead, is entirely coincidental.

AVON BOOKS
An Imprint of Harper Collins*Publishers*
10 East 53rd Street
New York, New York 10022-5299

ISBN: 0-380-81686-5
www.avonmystery.com

First Avon Books paperback printing: May 2004
First William Morrow hardcover printing: July 2003

Printed in the U.S.A.

10 9 8 7 6 5 4 3

This one's long overdue for
The Friday Night Adoption Society

Alice
Gretchen
Becky
Phoebe
Don
Melissa
Vern
Findlay
Meg
Robert
and
all the rest

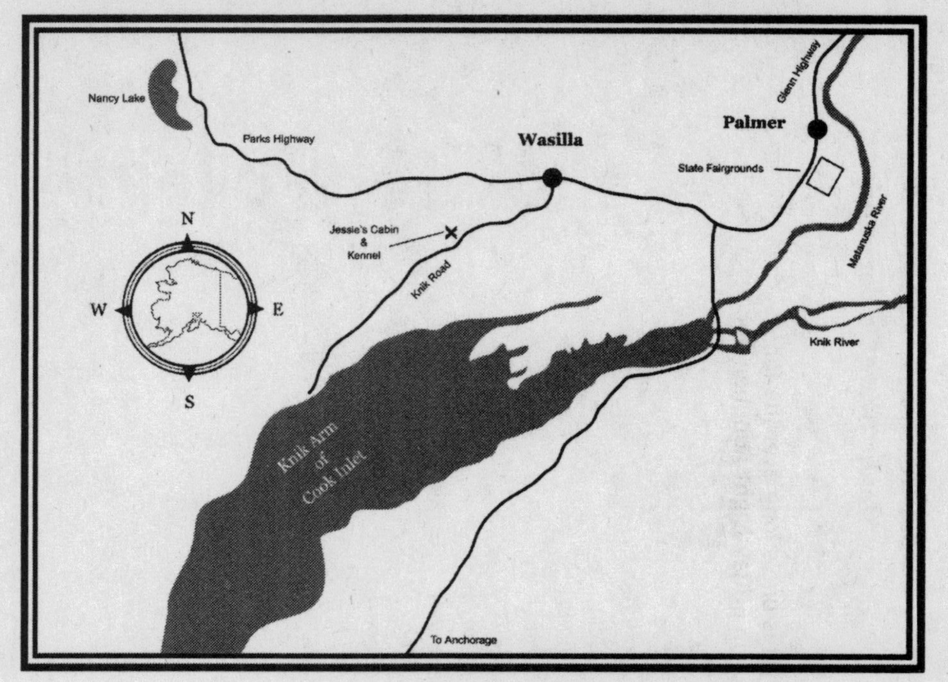

Nancy Lake
Parks Highway
Wasilla
Palmer
Glenn Highway
State Fairgrounds
Matanuska River
Jessie's Cabin
&
Kennel
Knik Road
N
W
E
S
Knik River
Knik Arm
of
Cook Inlet
To Anchorage

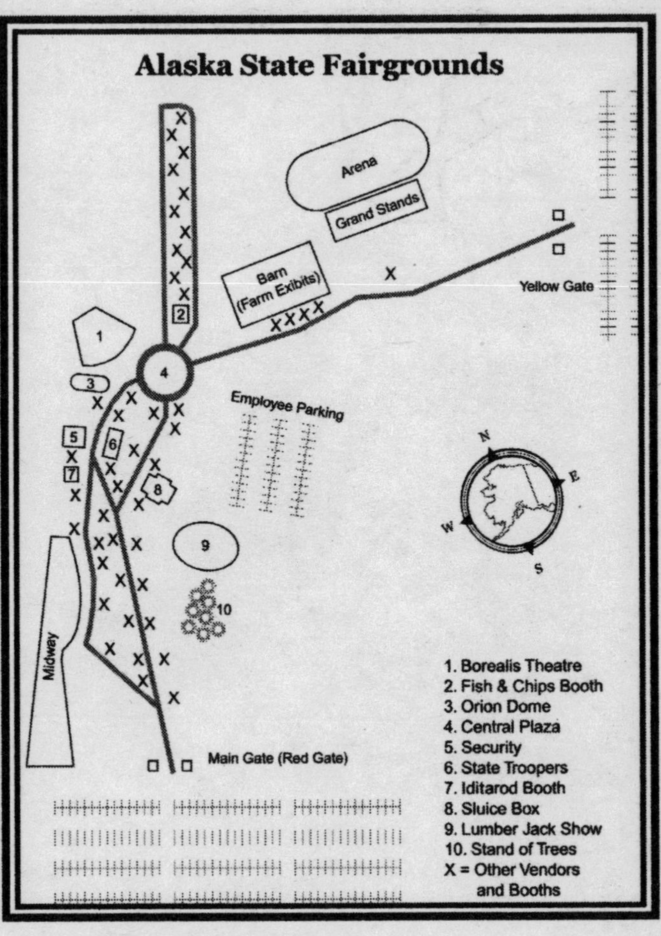
Alaska State Fairgrounds
Arena
Grand Stands
Barn
(Farm Exibits)
Yellow Gate
Employee Parking
Midway
Main Gate (Red Gate)
N
E
W
S
1. Borealis Theatre
2. Fish & Chips Booth
3. Orion Dome
4. Central Plaza
5. Security
6. State Troopers
7. Iditarod Booth
8. Sluice Box
9. Lumber Jack Show
10. Stand of Trees
X = Other Vendors
and Booths

DEATH TRAP

CHAPTER 1

I wasn't here then," he reminded her. "So now that it's all over, will you please explain to me just what you were doing by yourself in that dog yard at Nancy Lake."

Jessie Arnold frowned at the trooper's question, narrowed her gray eyes, and a curl of honey-blond hair fell over her forehead as she shook her head, remembering. As all eyes turned toward her, she shifted a bit self-consciously in her place on the big sofa that had been a housewarming gift for her new cabin. She glanced around the group of people that had gathered for dinner and now sat companionably in her living room, drinking coffee or beer and discussing the circumstances in which they had all, in one way or another, found themselves involved in the preceding few days.

Two were finishing a second slice of pie, and one had lit an aromatic pipe, adding a faint fruity scent to the pleasant smell of the fire in the potbellied iron stove. The fire crackled suddenly in the ensuing silence, which was broken again as Alaska State Trooper Phil Becker set his bottle of Killian's on its stone hearth with a clink. Crossing his arms on the back of the straight chair he straddled, he rested his chin on them and looked across at Jessie, waiting to see what she would say and attempting, though not very hard, to hide the I-told-you-so grin that twitched his lips.

"Better answer the question," he suggested finally.

"Oh, cut it out, Phil," she told him, attempting to look severe and failing. "We all know you think I shouldn't have gone off on my own, and you're probably right. But I was worried and angry, and it seemed a perfectly reasonable thing to do at the time. How was I to know . . ." She let the sentence trail off thoughtfully.

He shrugged, waiting for her to finish her defensive justification, but quit trying to control the grin and allowed it to spread across his face.

"I was looking for Tank," she began, turning to her questioner and ignoring Phil's expression.

At the sound of his name, Jessie's lead dog, Tank, sat up from where he was curled next to young Danny Tabor on the braided rug at her feet, all his attention focused on her face. She leaned forward and took the dog's face between both her hands and smiled as she spoke to him.

"Yes, I was looking for you. And found you, thank God, though it got us both into a lot of trouble."

He leaned blissfully into her caresses and gave her arm a lick, returning the affection.

"Lie down, good boy," she told him, and waited to continue her explanation till he had done so and laid his muzzle on Danny's knee.

"First, Maxie McNabb stopped by on her way to Colorado and—"

"Who's Maxie McNabb?" Danny asked.

Jessie sighed. Explaining everything that had happened was obviously not going to be easy.

"Maxie is a friend of mine who lives in Homer, but she travels to warmer places in her motor home during the winter. I met her when I drove a Winnebago up the Alaska Highway last May for Vic Prentice, the contractor who built this new cabin for me. She was coming back to Homer for the summer, and we ran into each other in a Canadian campground. We kept in touch, then in August she stopped here for a visit she had promised me on her way back to the Lower Forty-eight. It was a short visit, but our conversation gave me the idea of searching local dog yards, so that's where I went.

"I had gone to the fair, you see . . ." she continued, remembering what had transpired on her visit to one particular and unpleasant dog yard, and the situation in which she had found herself as a result.

The grin faded from Phil Becker's face. He listened intently, along with the circle of old and new friends who made up Jessie's audience, for there were details of what had happened that he had not yet heard and a few questions of his own to be answered.

Except for her voice and some gentle Celtic harp music from her sound system in the background, it was quiet in the room as the story began to unfold. Remembering how events had occurred, Jessie began to take herself back to that particular day and where she had found herself—and Tank.

CHAPTER 2

How did you get separated from Tank in the first place? He usually goes everywhere you do."

"Yes, he does," Jessie agreed. "But we were at the fair for the second day, and I wanted to take a look at the animals in the barn. I knew they wouldn't want a dog in there, so I left him with Joanne at the Iditarod booth for an hour. When I came back he was gone, and she was frantic. Then we searched everywhere, but—"

"You haven't said how you wound up at the fair in the first place," Becker interrupted. "Why don't you go back to when it all first began—when Joanne asked you to help."

Jessie nodded, visualizing the morning of the phone call. "Okay. I had just come back from a walk when she called. I couldn't work with my mutts—doctor's orders—and I'd been thinking I'd go crazy if I didn't find something to keep me busy."

She grew quiet for a minute, allowing events to order themselves in her mind. It had started so innocently—with a reasonable response to the plea of a good friend for assistance and the anticipation of a few days of enjoyable interaction with old and new sled dog racing fans.

"I took my morning coffee outside," she told the assembled group. "It was the first time I'd been able to smell fall in the air—a hint of cool air and dry leaves. You know. I stood there looking out at the yard where my dogs usually are, feeling frustrated. Then . . ."

With care not to slosh the hot coffee she carried in a blue pottery mug, Jessie stepped onto the porch of her new log cabin, closed the door behind her, and stood assessing the clearing that held her home and dog yard just off Knik Road a few miles west of Wasilla, Alaska. The last Saturday in August had dawned bright and clear at just before seven that morning, with a coolness in the air and the scent of drying grasses, reminding her that the ground in the nearby birch grove would soon be littered with leaves of gold. The drop in temperature raised a little steam from the coffee, which tickled her nose as she sipped it, cupping both hands around the mug, appreciating its warmth.

Except for the twitter of a small bird or two, it was quiet, an unusual state, as she was ordinarily greeted by barks and yelps from the occupants of her kennel, and one that left her with a restless sense of disquiet as she looked out at the almost empty yard. It seemed inexplicable that only a few of the more than forty dogs she owned were currently occupying their boxes; that the whole yard was not full of active, enthusiastic canines ready to continue fall training as soon as snow fell and grew deep enough to support a sled. But the majority of them had been taken to spend the winter with Lynn Ehlers, a friend who would add them to his own teams for training runs and races. It left Jessie with little to do at a time of year that was usually filled with preparation that raised her spirits in anticipation of the racing season.

Irritated with the situation and her enforced idleness, she swung too quickly toward the rocking chair where she intended to sit and felt a twinge of pain in the knee she had injured two months earlier in a fall down the steep side of a mountain. The tendon she had torn enough to require surgery was healing well, and she was no longer wearing a brace, but the doctor had cautioned against sled dog racing.

"If you're wise," he had solemnly advised her, with a penetrating look over the rims of his glasses, "you'll give it a rest this year, Jessie. If you don't compromise now, you'll be able to race next year without it bothering you unduly. I can't promise that if you don't. So no training runs or heavy kennel work, okay? And don't overdo the therapy."

She reluctantly agreed and had conscientiously kept to her prescribed regimen of physical exercise. But she had not realized how much her frustration level would rise when the leaves began to gild the birches of her woods. When the wind had delivered the first chill hint of fall and the nights grew longer and darker, and especially when the sky was swept with northern lights, she had found herself pacing the confines of her cabin, yearning to be out and about, preparing for a winter filled with swift teams of dogs and runs through the hushed and frozen wilds of her adopted state. Though she knew the situation was temporary, it was still an agonizing one that was difficult to accept and overcome.

Good thing I live alone, she thought, bending to rub at the knee with her knuckles. *No one else could put up with me right now.*

Hearing her slight intake of breath at the complaint in her knee, Tank, who had followed her out the door, pricked his ears attentively.

"Hey, boy."

Crossing the porch, she eased into the chair and, as he came to sit beside her, reached to massage his neck and shoulders. He laid his head on her good knee and leaned into the attention of her affectionate fingers.

"I should have sent you off with Lynn and the rest of my guys. You're getting as out of shape and lazy as I am."

But she knew they were a pair. He might need more activity than he would get this winter, but neither of them would benefit from a separation, so she had elected to keep him at home. The bond between them was strong and had been established through much more than the thousands of miles of running they had done together over the years.

"Well," she told him, more brightly than she felt, "we can at least take a walk, can't we?"

At the word, he wheeled and headed for the steps that led down to the yard. Looking back over his shoulder, he gave her such an eager doggy grin that she had to chuckle as she stood up and opened the cabin door to grab a sweater and shrug it on.

As they went down the front steps together, the few dogs left in the yard raised their heads or sat up where they had been resting in or near their boxes. Lack of activity had dulled their usual optimistic expectation of exercise, and they exhibited a decided lack of enthusiasm, though they had been interested enough in the food and water she had provided for them earlier.

They don't expect me to take them out, Jessie realized sadly, or they'd be tugging at their tethers and yelping for attention.

Only one of the older dogs, who like Jessie was nursing an almost healed injury, responded to the appearance of woman and lead dog by pacing toward them and attentively watching Jessie's face with longing in his eyes.

"Good old Pete."

She walked across to lean down, rub his ears, and unfasten his tether. "You want to come with us? Why not?"

She stood for a moment looking toward Knik Road, which ran past the end of her long driveway, then frowned and headed for the woods behind her cabin instead. On a day as full of approaching fall as this, with the bite of cooler temperatures in the air to inspire them, other mushers would be out with their teams on training runs. Until there was snow and it grew deep enough to fill the woodland trails, they would drive their dogs ahead of four-wheel ATVs on trails that paralleled Knik Road, and she had no desire to meet them and to see the sympathy in their eyes and voices at finding her afoot, still limping slightly.

Circling the cabin, she led Pete and Tank to a narrow cut in the trees that would lead eventually to a whole network of training trails that ran for miles in all directions, maintained by the sled dog racers who had created them and used them every winter. Without snow to cover the tangles of groundcover, stumps of small trees and bushes had been hacked off and removed, along with the summer's growth of weeds. It was a path too rough for training but suitable for walking if she watched her footing and took care not to stumble. She could stroll at a comfortable pace, accommodate the limitations of her injury, and enjoy her two mutts' delight in freedom from leash or harness.

The woods were fairly quiet, some of the small birds that filled them with a cheerful summer cacophony already fleeing south before the frost arrived with chill winds to snatch leaves from the trees to litter the ground. A few leaves already crunched beneath her feet, and their earthy, slightly acrid smell rose in a pungent reminder of damp and decay to blend with a pale scent of wood smoke on the breeze from some neighbor's breakfast fire.

As Jessie paused to examine the rose hips plumping on a bush beside the trail, a squirrel chattered noisily down from the bare limb of a nearby birch at the three trespassers in its territory. Tank and Pete both hesitated and raised their heads at the sound but, wise to the improbability of catching such a scold, immediately moved on and ignored the challenge. Pinching off one of the rose hips, Jessie rolled it between her fingers and considered gathering a pocketful to dry and save for tea rich with vitamin C. The idea was tempting, but knowing she didn't really care all that much for the brew, she decided to leave them alone. Some moose would relish these later in the year. The extreme plumpness of the bright red berrylike fruit reminded her that they were supposed to be an indication of a heavy winter.

From somewhere close a raven called from high above her head but, though she carefully inspected the treetops, remained a disembodied sound. Three times it broke the stillness of the woods with its ragged croak before taking flight, a soaring black silhouette against the thin cloud cover of the sky. Hearing the raven reminded Jessie that, according to legend, this trickster of the northern world had once had a lovely singing voice and pure white feathers but had lost them both in flames cast by an angry magician from whom it had craftily stolen the sun, moon, and stars. The heat had charred it black and left it with only the scorched croak; one of the many raven tales that always made her smile.

For over an hour, the three enjoyed the freedom of the woods. Slowly the overcast cleared and sunshine brightened and warmed the morning with long shafts of light that splashed down through the canopy of the branches. Jessie's mood lifted, and she found herself humming in wordless appreciation of the world around her. It was good sometimes to wander slowly along and notice the many small things that would soon be buried in snow. On a sled, behind a dog team, they all vanished in a blur of speed. Fall was her favorite season, and it was pleasant to have time to enjoy it, even if that gratification was the result of losing her usual training runs.

Tank and Pete, who had been ranging widely in the surrounding woods, examining everything they found, gamboling through the brush like half-grown pups, leaping over logs and chasing each other, now returned to where Jessie had lowered herself to a stump to watch their performance. They sat down together in front of her like a pair of bookends, panting with exertion.

"You're a couple of fakers and clowns," she told them affectionately, elbows on knees, chin cupped in the palms of her hands to bring her face closer to their level. Pete reached up to give her nose a sloppy lick, which made her laugh. "Had enough? Shall we go home?"

Evidently they had, for when she stood up, they headed back the way they had come, toward the cabin and dog yard, walking slowly now, content to keep her company.

The yard, when they reached it, was just as she had left it. Jessie fastened Pete and Tank to their tethers and watched as they thirstily lapped the water in their pans. As soon as they were satisfied, they lay down on the straw that covered the floor of their boxes, ready for a nap.

Jessie turned to watch a pickup pass on Knik Road, and the sight of the mailbox at that end of her drive reminded her that it was time to collect whatever the postman had left her, if anything. Slowly she walked the length of the drive, avoiding several puddles that would soon be iced over, and pulled a scant handful of letters and bills from the box, along with a Snickers bar, which brought a grin to her face. With the mail, Ted the postman periodically left a treat from the stash he carried on his appointed rounds, and clearly he had figured out her preference in sweets.

Tucking the mail under one arm and peeling back the paper on the candy, she took a bite and, relishing the meld of chocolate, caramel, and nuts, hesitated a minute to look around before heading back up the drive. But there were no vehicles on the road, and nothing moved in the clearing to attract her attention. It seemed very empty, and a sudden sense of isolation brought a wrinkle to her forehead. Everyone she knew who wasn't busy with dogs was involved in winterizing houses and cabins to make sure the cold stayed outside where it belonged. Even those chores were not waiting for her this year. The summer had been filled with the construction of a brand-new cabin that was solid and winter-proof. It was also unusually neat and orderly, for though housework was never her occupation of choice and her living space was always comfortably cluttered, with plenty of time on her hands she had seized upon every small chore available.

Slowly Jessie walked back along the drive. Tank and Pete were both snoozing, but Tank opened an eye to watch her pass. She climbed the steps and went inside, where she took off her sweater, then headed for the kitchen to put the kettle on for tea, munching the last bite of the postman's largesse.

This is ridiculous, she thought as she waited for the water to boil. *There's gotta be something I can do to keep from going stark raving mad.*

Tea steaming in her favorite cup, she settled on the sofa by the stove to open the handful of envelopes she had retrieved. But before she could do more than sort out and discard the junk mail, the phone rang, and she dropped the rest to cross the room in response.

"Arnold Kennels."

The voice on the other end of the line was familiar and welcome—Joanne Potts, longtime friend and worker with the Iditarod Sled Dog Race.

"Hey, Joanne," Jessie greeted her, assuming she must be calling to ask why a registration for the race had not been filed. "You must have heard that I can't race this year."

"Yes—and I was sorry to hear it. But knowing you're not out training inspired me to call. I've got an unexpected problem you might be able to help with, if you would."

"What's up?" Jessie asked, hearing a plea in the woman's voice. *Be careful what you wish for*, crossed her mind, remembering what she had just told herself she wanted—something to keep from going bonkers.

"I'm suddenly short two people to help run our booth at the fair," Joanne told her in obvious frustration. "Virginia Williams is home sick, and Barbara Brosier had to make an emergency trip to Tuscaloosa, Alabama. I'm even taking care of both her dogs, including a Saint Bernard, and two cats, Cotton and Alley. Don't you love it? Alley cat! But as a result, right now I'm struggling down here by myself and thought you might be able to come down and help me out."

The fair! Jessie remembered. The annual Alaska State Fair had started the day before and would run another ten days, through Labor Day, at the grounds in Palmer. *How could I have forgotten?* she asked herself.

Her hesitation motivated her caller to another flood of words.

"You wouldn't have to be here all the time, or even for the whole week. But if you could help cover some of the busiest times, it would give me the opportunity to find another volunteer or two. Please, Jessie, I'm desperate!"

Well—why not?

She considered the physical limitations imposed by her injury. "Can I sit down part of the time? This knee gets tired, and I'm supposed to be letting it heal."

The answer was quick and positive. "Sure. Whatever you need. I'll even fetch you coffee—feed you—almost anything. Yes?"

"Can I bring Tank?"

"You bet! I've got to sell a pile of lottery tickets and he'd be a great draw. You know how the public loves dogs."

Jessie gave in with a grin at the woman's assurances. "Okay, I'll do it. When do you want us?"

The relief in Joanne's answer carried clearly over the line. "Now! Yesterday! As soon as you can get here?"

"Give me an hour or so."

"Thanks a bunch. I hoped I could count on you." And she was gone, leaving Jessie to drop the phone back in its cradle, a sense of anticipation rising.

She loved the fair and went every year, usually more than once. But she had never helped out and would now have a chance to see how it worked from the inside. Besides, having run the Iditarod several times in the past, she felt identification with the race and was inclined to support it in any way she could.

This'll be fun, she thought, turning her attention to what needed to be done before she could leave.

What could possibly not be fun about the Alaska State Fair?

She had no way of knowing that the answer to such an assumption would not be long in coming.

CHAPTER 3

"That was the day you ran into me, right?" Ten-year-old Danny Tabor looked up at Jessie from his place on the floor at her feet.

"Yes, but I didn't get to know you till later."

"When I came to visit Tank at the booth."

Phil Becker interrupted their exchange with a recommendation. "You better tell how you got to the fair, Danny."

"Aw, do I have to?"

"I think you should. It's a significant part of the story."

"Well—okay." He wiggled a little in embarrassment, sat up straighter, and took a deep breath. "It was because I forgot to mow the lawn . . ."

"I'm not going to tell you again, Danny."

The woman, her arms half to the elbows in a sink full of dirty dishes, cast an aggravated glance over her shoulder at the boy who stood glowering in the kitchen doorway, wiped perspiration from her forehead with one arm, and sighed in frustration.

"Your father said you couldn't go, and he's not going to change his mind. You'd *better* get the lawn mowed before he comes home for lunch."

"Yeah, but it's not fair I can't go. I saved my allowance all summer."

"You should have thought of that yesterday."

"But when I get it mowed, *then* can I go?"

"Not this weekend. You've also got summer reading homework—that book report you're supposed to have for Miss Carson at the library on Monday. You haven't even finished the book."

"It's a boring book."

"You liked *Treasure Island*."

"That had pirates and treasure. This is just some old guy stuck on an island. Bor-ing."

"Everything can't have pirates. *Robinson Crusoe* is a fine book."

Danny glared through the strands of light brown hair that fell over his eyes and, as persistent as he was angry, tossed them back, pounded an impotent fist against the frame of the door, and allowed a wheedling tone to creep into his voice. "Ple-e-eze let me go, Ma."

"No!" she told him without turning. "Give it up, Danny. It's your own fault and . . ."

"Dammit!" he interrupted and, advancing two strides into

the kitchen, kicked the leg of a chair, making it—and his mother—jump. Incensed, she swung around to raise a warning hand in his direction, flinging water and soapsuds onto the floor between them.

"Don't you *dare* swear at me! You'll—"

But realizing he had pushed his mother past her limits of sympathy or tolerance, Danny had already vanished. She heard the door to his room slam behind him.

Now he'll lock himself in and sulk, she thought in irritated discouragement, returning to the task at hand. *Well, at least he won't be whining at me.* It worried her that her son didn't like to read and was slow at it. His teacher had suggested in a parent conference that he would need remedial help if he was not to be held back a year in school. Adding summer reading, even when she and his father worked with him, was creating tension between the boy and his parents. He tended to resist, often disappearing when it was time to read.

But Danny had no intention of sulking. Visions of the dizzying spin of carnival rides, plus all the hot dogs, popcorn, and sodas he could afford to ingest, filled his mind and whetted his appetite. He could almost taste the sticky texture of cotton candy melting on his tongue. There would be Chinese acrobats, skateboard exhibitions, and booths full of all kinds of tempting stuff. Last year he had come home with colorful plastic streamers for the handlebars of his bicycle, spinners for its wheels, and an inflatable pink flamingo for his little sister. Rebellious grievance and anger at his parents, especially his father, fueled his determination to spend the day with his two best buddies at the Alaska State Fair.

"Bet *he* forgot to mow the lawn sometimes," he muttered to himself as he leaned back against the door he had slammed and locked behind him.

Checking to make sure it was secure, he stood for a minute making up his mind and building courage. Decision stubbornly made, he squared his shoulders, marched across to the CD player on the top shelf of a corner bookcase, and adjusted the volume upward. Grabbing the jeans jacket and backpack he had earlier stashed under his bed, he raised the window that led to the backyard. Quietly unlatching and raising the screen, he dropped the backpack to the ground beneath, yanked on his jacket, and crawled out. Once there, he glanced around warily to make sure none of the neighbors had observed his unusual egress, then trotted to the rear of the garage, where he had conveniently left his bicycle. Tossing the backpack over a handlebar, he pedaled off across a vacant lot toward a Palmer side street, taking care to keep the garage between himself and the kitchen window.

Jessie had listened to his account with an encouraging hand on his shoulder. When he paused to take a sip of his soda, she gave him an approving pat, then smiled and turned her attention to another of the company that had gathered in her living room for the evening.

"You weren't the only one who ran away from home. We should hear from Mr. Monroe, too."

Directly across the room, an older gentleman was comfortably ensconced in an overstuffed chair, feet on a pillowed stool, glass of Guinness in one hand. It was apparent from the twinkle of humor in his eye and his courtly nod in her direction that he was fond of Jessie. "You said you'd call me Frank," he reminded her.

"Yes, sir." She beamed back at him.

"It's true that I played truant," he agreed. "But I postulate that it would be more accurate to say that I ran away from the grocery store. And I took a taxi, not a bicycle—much more efficient, as it dropped me off right at the gate."

Jessie had grown used to Monroe's rather eccentric way of speaking, but considering the grin that twitched Becker's lips and Danny's puzzled expression, his use of large words clearly amused and startled more than one of his audience.

"What's pos—ah—pos-oo-late mean?" Danny asked.

"Pos-tu-late. It means 'to assume' or 'to claim'—really 'to suggest' something," Monroe told him. "I suggest that it's more correct to say that I ran away from the grocery store than from home. Okay?"

Danny nodded. "Pos-tu-late," he repeated. "Thanks."

His mother gave him a slightly bemused and approving look, surprised at his interest in what the word meant.

Monroe, catching her eye, gave her a wink and launched into his tale of escape.

At approximately the same time Danny was crawling out his bedroom window, across town at the Palmer Senior Center for Assisted Living, eighty-two-year-old Frank Monroe was contriving a similar escape, though climbing out a window was not a part of his strategy. His flight plan was of a more complex and opportunistic nature.

He slipped on his favored and well-worn tweed sports jacket over the light blue shirt he was already wearing, then cupped one of the suede elbow patches in the palm of his hand, enjoying the soft familiar texture for a moment. As he stepped to the mirror to attend to his tie, the door of his room burst open to reveal a chunky female figure clad in a tunic printed solidly with cats in a rainbow of colors.

"Hurry it up, Frankie. The van is waiting and you're holding up the parade."

The nurse supervisor carried a red pencil in one hand, with which she checked off his name on her clipboard list, then stood waiting, an impatient frown drawing her bushy eyebrows even closer to the visible mustache on her upper lip. Her entrance, unannounced by a knock, as usual, had startled Monroe into dropping the clip with which he had been about to anchor his tie.

"Did I miss your knock, Miss Richards?" he inquired, bending to retrieve it and giving her a resentful glance in the mirror as he took his time to make sure the clip was centered before inserting the attached chain through a shirt buttonhole. "Must have neglected to turn up my hearing aid again."

Ignoring Monroe's sarcastic comment, she opened the door wider and indicated with an abrupt gesture that he was to precede her through it.

Didn't nurses wear white anymore? He speculated for a fleeting moment on her inclination to chose a print that emphasized her physical bulk, decided against asking, and retrieved his cane and ancient leather knapsack from the foot of the bed. From atop the chest of drawers he plucked his gray hat, jaunty green feather in the band, settled it at a slightly rakish angle, and gave himself a nod of approval in the mirror. Better to remain malleable and obedient, today of all days.

"Come *on,* Frankie boy," she demanded.

Monroe, with a sigh of resignation, sidled past her and waited as she closed the door. Following her down the hallway toward the lobby, he considered his dissatisfaction with Nurse Ratchet, as he had privately dubbed her—stealing the name from *One Flew Over the Cuckoo's Nest*—and the majority of the rest of the staff at the Palmer Senior Center for Assisted Living.

Buxom Doris Richards, Monroe mused, could have modeled for the figurehead of some eighteenth-century sailing ship, probably British. As a figurehead, she would at least have been silent. But he imagined she would undoubtedly have attempted to organize the fleet and teach Nelson a thing or two had she been available for consultation before the Battle of Trafalgar. Nelson, however, would probably not have tolerated her overbearing superiority and didactic attitude, though she might well have whipped the French and Spanish into surrender in record time, given the opportunity.

The word *harridan* came to mind. *Why couldn't the woman* ever *knock*? The door, to his infinite regret, was unlockable. And though he kept it closed, most of the staff ignored the implication, coming and going as though it didn't exist.

Complaints to the administrator were useless. She had

set her elbows on her desk and made a steeple of her fingers, through which she smiled with fraudulent concern. "We have to have access, Mr. Monroe. What if you had another stroke or a heart attack, and we were unable to reach you quickly? We're responsible for you now. You must understand that."

It had only been a small warning stroke—hardly a hiccup. Even the doctor said so. But it had cost Monroe his driver's license and precious mobility. Otherwise he was perfectly able to care for himself and, like most senior citizens, cherished his independence. But called upon to provide essential transportation one afternoon a week, his nephew had begun to suggest that he should sell his house and move to an apartment within walking distance of a grocery and pharmacy. When he refused, the term *assisted living* arose in conversation, and a variety of unwelcome brochures began to clutter his mailbox, extolling the virtues of a succession of what Monroe disparaged as *pigeonholes for the almost dead.*

Two minor incidents and the threat of a competency hearing had altered his point of view.

The first had transpired the preceding February, when he slipped on the return from his mailbox and found himself unable to regain his footing on the icy surface of his walk. A passing neighbor had observed him—mail clenched in his teeth, crawling steadily toward the house, amused at the situation and his own plight—and felt it necessary not only to come to his rescue but to inform his nephew.

The second incident had involved a stove burner, his ancient teakettle, and an after-dinner nap. The smoke alarm had awakened Monroe to a hot petroleum smell and sent him stumbling to the kitchen in apprehension and with all possible haste. There he found that heat from the glowing electric burner had melted the spout off the teakettle, which had tumbled to scorch a scar into the Formica countertop, filling the air with noxious fumes. A twist of the burner control and a cup of water quickly cooled the neglected source of heat. But the smell was impossible to disguise or get rid of before his nephew appeared the next afternoon. Discovery of the charred spot in the Formica and the teakettle in the trash had inspired the competency threat.

Weary of defending his autonomy, and secretly a bit alarmed at his own ineptitude, Monroe had given in to the point of a visit to a couple of the detested *pigeonholes*. From there it had become a slippery slope indeed. Very shortly he found himself installed at the Palmer Senior Center for Assisted Living, the equity from his property and meager savings invested in the promise of a *private* apartment with personal care he now knew the contract had euphemistically labeled *dignified*, as it included the unlockable door.

After six months, Monroe was exceedingly fed up with being treated as if he had lost his brains along with his liberty. As a retired history professor, he knew the value of treating people with respect; he had dealt with his students as adults who were responsible and accountable for their own learning. Appalled at the continued invasions of his privacy, he had finally had enough.

As he followed Nurse Richards out the front door to the

van, already half full of other venerable *prisoners of fortune*, the hint of a self-satisfied smile twitched his lips. Taking a seat by himself toward the rear of the van, he reassuringly patted the leather backpack and watched the streets of Palmer pass on the way to the local mall.

CHAPTER 4

When the van pulled up at the mall, Frank Monroe got out with the rest of the passengers, waiting patiently for Shirley Anders, who was nearly crippled with arthritis, to make her way down the steps. When she had finally descended to the sidewalk, he unfolded her walker for her. With a vague smile of thanks in his direction, she turned to make her way laboriously through the automatic doors of the supermarket. Monroe followed her in, glancing back to find Nurse Richards watching like a hawk as her flock scattered, intent on keeping track of them.

"You have half an hour, Frankie," she reminded him sharply.

He ignored her, picked up a basket, and headed for the pharmacy in the rear of the store, where he wanted to have the prescription for his blood pressure pills refilled. He made sure to use the cane he didn't really need and to walk slowly as he moved away from her. As soon as a quick right turn took him down an aisle out of her sight, he tucked the cane under one arm and picked up his pace considerably.

Halfway along it, he snatched a bottle of water from a shelf and dropped it in the basket without stopping. It took only a minute or two to locate the soda crackers two aisles away, and on impulse he took a box of gingersnaps as well. Was there anything else on his mental list? Doubling back, he added a couple of small cans of Vienna sausages.

Even with her walker, Shirley Anders had beaten him to the pharmacy, along with two other *pigeonhole* residents. They stood chatting as they waited for their prescriptions, completely blocking the counter.

"Excuse me, ladies," Monroe apologized, reaching between them to set his basket on the counter. "Coming through."

They shifted enough to let him follow his basket and give his name to the pharmacist, who gave him a smile and reached to a shelf behind her for Monroe's pills. He had been wise enough to call ahead, saving himself precious minutes of valuable time.

"Want me to ring this up, too?" She indicated the items in the basket as he signed the record book.

"Please." He handed her a bill, took the plastic bag that now held his grocery items, and started to turn away.

"Don't forget your change, Mr. Monroe," she called, holding it out.

"Having a senior moment, Frankie?" From directly behind him, Nurse Richards's voice held a note of sarcasm.

Jamming the change into a pants pocket, he frowned at his own stupidity in forgetting it and attracting her attention.

Swinging around, he confronted her. "No. I was just in a hurry. Half an hour isn't long enough, you know."

The very thought raised his ire. He liked to browse the aisles at the grocery store, or any store for that matter. How could he know what he wanted until he saw what was offered? And why couldn't they go to a hardware store for a change, where there were hundreds of interesting things to discover, even if he had no particular use for them?

As he frowned at her, Doris Richards suddenly reached to pull open the plastic bag he was holding and examine what he had just purchased. "Hm-m. Lot of carbohydrates and sugar there. You'd better get some roughage and vitamin C in your snacks, Frankie."

Suddenly furious, he yanked the bag from her presumptuous, meddlesome fingers and stomped off toward the produce section of the store, completely forgetting to use the cane. *Apples!* He had meant to pick up apples and a couple of oranges. It galled him that it had taken Nurse Ratchet to remind him.

When he had selected two apples, he held them and hesitated. Damn. Now he would have to go back to the front of the store to pay for them—or would he? He took a look at his watch. Ten minutes left before Ratchet started rounding up stragglers.

"Oh, get the hell on with it," he muttered in exasperation.

He hadn't shoplifted anything since he was a kid, but he hadn't forgotten how. Seeing only one produce employee neatly arranging celery and no one else close enough to see, he held the plastic bag behind a counter and dropped in the apples. Heading for the back of the section, he added oranges on the fly as he passed a bin of them. Pausing in front of another bin next to the pair of swinging doors through which produce came and went, he picked up a tomato and pretended to be examining it as he glanced carefully around. This part was critical.

The produce section was empty of customers, and the celery arranger had turned his back when Frank Monroe slipped through the swinging doors into the shadowy recesses of the back of the store, taking the tomato with him. *In for a penny,* he thought as he made his way down the narrow aisles between piles of crates and boxes to a rear door, opened it, and found himself in the parking lot, exactly where he had expected to be.

Fifty yards across it was a Chevron station with a pay phone link to a taxi. With just a little luck, he could be gone before they figured out that he was not wandering somewhere in the store. "Or before they can find and arrest me for shoplifting," he told himself with a grin, and stepped out smartly toward his goal.

Let them all stew—especially Ratchet. The state fair was only a few miles away, and he intended to be there shortly to enjoy it.

So you met Jess at the Iditarod booth, Frank?"

"No—I observed her that afternoon in her collision with young Danny. But I didn't meet her on that particular day."

Jessie leaned forward on the sofa in eager recollection. "That's right. I'd forgotten. You were sitting on a bench and tipped your hat to me."

"I did indeed, and you waved back. I knew who you were—watched you race on the television. I thought you handled the result of the pirate encounter very well."

"I'd taken a break for lunch," she recalled. "And speaking of breaks, let's suspend the story long enough to refill drinks and move around a little."

Almost everyone stood up and began to talk to each other, or headed for the kitchen or bathroom, but Jessie hesitated by Frank Monroe's chair. "It could have been better circumstances, but I'm so glad I met you," she told him. "Are things any better at the Palmer Center?"

He cocked an eyebrow wickedly and gave her a self-satisfied smile. "I've made it a challenge," he said. "I've taken to periodically propping a chair under the door handle. Doesn't exclude them from my room entirely, but it's an impediment with which they'd rather not struggle. Though remarkably colorful in language and laggard in acquiring new habits, most of the staff have now mastered the ability to knock."

"If I didn't know better, I'd suspect that you're enjoying yourself," Jessie said, amused.

"You could be right," he agreed. "And to top it off, I lobbied for more time at the grocery. Nurse Ratchet is now forced to wait for an hour."

Jessie couldn't resist teasing. "No more shoplifting?"

He shook his head, the eyebrow once again figuring in his expression. "I must admit, however, that at the time it was refreshing—made me feel young."

"You should have lived a long time ago, when you *could have been a pirate."*

They both laughed.

"Get settled," he encouraged. "I have yet to hear the end of this tale and more of your part should come soon, I believe."

At two o'clock that first afternoon at the fair, Jessie sat at a picnic table not far from the Iditarod booth, taking a break for a late lunch and watching crowds of attendees stream past her. The general commotion of the fair was as entertaining as the displays or events on its printed roster, and she enjoyed being an observer as the endless crowd moved around her. Tank lay at her feet beneath the table, content to retreat from the excess of attention he had been receiving throughout the day from adults and children alike. As Joanne Potts had predicted, a lead dog that had guided a sled all the way to Nome was a great draw. While Joanne sold raffle tickets for a bright red Dodge pickup, Jessie answered questions about sled dog racing and sold Iditarod shirts, pins, and posters, autographing one that featured her and her team. There had been little time to rest her knee, so she was glad to sit down and be a spectator.

It was a sunny day with a few clouds over the spectacular Chugach Mountains that framed the MatSu Valley to the east and south, Pioneer Peak rising sharply against the sky. Area residents, including Jessie, were so used to living next door to wilderness that they seldom noticed it as they went about their daily lives. Now, for a moment, it struck her that there were probably no other fairgrounds with such an impressive setting. Yet no one she could see so much as raised a glance toward the natural panorama surrounding them. All focused on the pleasures of the fair.

There was certainly enough to retain that focus. Music and shrieks from the midway provided a background for the babble of dozens of passing voices and the blare of a loudspeaker announcing an upcoming skateboard event. From a sound system somewhere came snatches of a tune that Jessie could almost, but not quite, recognize. The smells of popcorn and hot sugar from a cotton candy machine drifted temptingly on the breeze from nearby booths, enhanced with the scent of barbecue from another. Ribs wouldn't be a bad idea for dinner later, she thought, and made a mental note to remember to pick some up before she left for home.

From where she sat, she could see people pouring in through the west gate, picking up daily schedules from a kiosk, and wandering along the walkways, immediately entranced with the colorful booths and exhibits. A red barn near the entrance announced an ANTIQUE SHOW—SALE NOW! Next to it was parked a blue truck with the NBC rainbow peacock logo on the side and a large satellite dish on the roof—the local Channel 2 News command center. Not far away was another truck, white this time, bearing the Wells Fargo stagecoach and horses and simply labeled ATM. Jessie imagined a parent with several hungry children who would probably make themselves sick on the whirling rides and have to be fed all over again when their stomachs settled back to earth.

Besides being a money pit, the fair was a kaleidoscope of

bright colors, from the midway flags to a nearby display of oversized suckers and sugary spirals on long sticks. With the sun behind it, the candy practically glowed against the brilliant red background of a protective canvas. Balloons, banners, and streamers bobbed and floated in the breeze. Jessie grinned to see that one vendor at least had taken personal advantage of the hair-dying booth. Standing at the door of his leather goods booth, he smiled and waved as he saw her looking. His long hair had been combed and sprayed into spikes that stood out from his head, each spike a different color, beard done to match in magenta, yellow, and blue. Next door, a long, narrow booth announced its inventory on a bright yellow sign that read ROCKS, FOSSILS & OTHER NEAT STUFF.

As she contemplated a quick trip to discover what *neat stuff* meant, her attention was drawn to two mothers passing. One was pushing a toddler in a stroller, the other pulling two older children in a red Radio Flyer wagon across the back of which someone had written *Kiddy Limo* with a felt-tip marker. Both the children, a boy of four or five and his slightly younger brother, had also had their hair temporarily dyed bright colors—one green and blue, the other red and orange. It stuck out from their heads as if they had been swept up with a rainbow in a whirlwind. Neither looked particularly happy. They sat as far away from each other as they could get, considering the limitations of the wagon, giving Jessie the impression they were no longer sure they were related. Watching them disappear into the crowd, she thought it likely the dye job had been their mother's idea, not theirs.

Long lines of people waiting for a turn on the carnival rides had encouraged Jessie to give that part of the fair a pass for the time being, though she would have liked to ride the Ferris wheel. From the top she would be able to see the whole fair spread out below. A quick assessment from the entrance to the midway showed her that the Tilt-a-Whirl and Ferris wheel were popular with parents of the younger set, while older kids sprinted past them, inclined toward more thrilling adventures in speed and centrifugal force.

Finished with the gyro she had purchased at a nearby stall, Jessie stood up from the table, wadded the wrapper, now soaked with the residue of sour cream, onions, and cucumber, tossed it into a trash can, and wiped her hands on her jeans. Joanne had said to take her time, so with Tank's leash firmly in hand, she strolled east along the paved walkway between the stalls to see what might be new and interesting this year.

A colorful display of fabric caught her attention, and she stepped into a booth filled with flags, banners, and piles of bandanas of every color and design imaginable. Selecting a bright orange one, she paid for it, then tied it around Tank's neck and smiled as he sat up a bit straighter, seeming to feel dashing and dressed up to match the bright swirl of colors around him.

"There. But I won't get you dyed to match, I promise."

Wandering on up the crowded walk, they soon came to the central plaza, a wide-open space where most of the walkways came together. In the center a sand sculptor was busy creating a replica of that year's fair logo. A cartoon moose in a space helmet had already been carved and peered out from under his visor toward the top of the pile of wet sand. The sculptor was busy with a trowel, removing excess sand to form the rest of the animal. He was perhaps Hawaiian, or at least from some warmer, sunnier latitude, for his legs below his Bermuda shorts were as deeply tanned as his face. Cooler northern weather had encouraged him to wear a sweatshirt, in contrast to most of the locals who were watching him work. Few of them had on anything heavier than a T-shirt, and several also wore shorts, but their legs were pale in comparison. Alaskans, according to a familiar saying, don't tan—they thaw.

Across the plaza, Jessie could see a huge barn labeled FARM EXHIBITS, which housed the livestock. She was tempted to take a look, but remembering that she had canine company, she decided to leave it for another day. As she swung around without warning to start back to the Iditarod booth, she ran flat into one of a trio of nine- or ten-year-old boys who were walking close behind her. In the general noise of the crowd, she had not heard their voices and was unaware of their presence until she almost knocked one of them over.

"Oops. Sorry," she said, reaching with her free hand to steady the boy she had met so abruptly, who was about to lose his balance and tumble backward onto the paved walk.

"Thanks." He looked up at her with a painted face. Probably done at the same booth that was also dying hair, she thought. Strands of light brown hair fell across his forehead and over his eyes, released from the black-and-white bandana that had slipped from his head to the ground in the encounter. He combed them back with his fingers, and Jessie could see that the cosmetic artist had made him a pirate, complete with a goatee, a handlebar mustache, and a black circle around one eye, so that when he blinked it appeared to be a patch.

"Good job on the face paint," she told him. "Who are you? Blackbeard?"

Any hint of a sinister seagoer was banished by his delighted grin. He grabbed the bandana, which Jessie could see was decorated with several appropriate skulls and crossbones, and yanked it back onto his head without untying its knots.

"Yeah," he agreed. "How'd you guess?"

"Come *on,* Danny," one of the other boys called from a few steps away.

"Bye," he told Jessie and moved to join his buddies, giving Tank a pat as he passed. "I like your dog," he tossed back, and the three disappeared into the crowd.

Fun to be a kid at a fair, Jessie mused and shared her amusement by smiling at an elderly man who had clearly observed the encounter from his seat on a nearby bench. With a wrinkled hand, he tipped the gray hat he was wearing, a perky green feather in the band, and gave her a gallant nod of greeting. *Or an old one, for that matter,* she decided as she gave him a wave and headed back toward another stint of greeting the public at the Iditarod booth.

She did not notice two men just entering the plaza from

another walkway, who had watched her encounter with the boy before turning their attention elsewhere.

But they did catch the notice of someone else as they stood speaking together in low voices and glancing around to be sure no one came close enough to overhear their conversation.

CHAPTER 5

I was still sitting on that bench," Frank Monroe continued the story, "when I saw two men behaving rather oddly."

Monroe watched Jessie walk away. When she disappeared, he turned his attention to the passing crowd and noticed two men who had also watched her as they strolled casually from one of the walkways that converged in the plaza. They ambled toward the sand sculptor, who had climbed down from his work and was packing his tools, finished for the day. The taller of the two wore a black T-shirt and baseball cap and carried a red gym bag over one shoulder. Reflective sunglasses covered the upper part of his face, and though he seemed to be examining the sculpture, his attention was actually directed toward something else.

"Over there," he spoke quietly, giving a quick nod to the

left. "That red building with the British flag on the front. You see?"

"It's a food booth. So?" said the shorter man, shoving one hand in a pocket of his blue windbreaker and scrubbing at his blond crew cut with the other.

"*Ye-ah.* One end's a food booth. But it's twice as big as they need to sell sausages and stuff, and there're no windows on that other end—just a heavy steel door with serious locks. Wadda ya think it's for?"

His companion looked up and frowned. "I don't know. You tell me."

"Don't be a dope, Curt. What have we been talking about?"

"Oh—the mon—"

"*Shut it!*" the taller man snapped, glancing around to see if anyone was near enough to overhear. "Here's the deal. My friend says that once every day, before the fair opens, an armored truck drives in through the south entrance and pulls up behind that place. A few minutes later it drives out again. What does that tell you?"

The shorter man raised the shoulders of his blue windbreaker ear-ward in a shrug. "I guess they pick up—"

"Good boy. You guess right," his pal interrupted, clapping him on the back with one hand. "Somewhere, locked up in the other end of that building," he muttered softly, "all night long, the whole day's receipts are . . ." He allowed his words to drift into silence, and a sly, self-satisfied grin twisted the corners of his mouth upward. Carefully he assessed the red building one last time, wishing he had X-ray vision and could see through walls. He would have liked to know exactly what kind of a safe was used to secure the huge amount of money the fair must generate each day, but it was a detail best left to the boss of this operation.

"But how're we gonna—"

Grabbing the shorter man's elbow in a grip that pinched hard enough to make him yip in protest, the man who seemed to be in charge pulled him across the plaza toward a walkway that ran past the red building in question.

"We can't stand here discussing this. Walk away, man, and I'll show you the pictures."

The taller one practically dragged the other one across the plaza, and they disappeared to the east," Monroe explained. "Unfortunately, it wasn't their last appearance. Danny and I were later to more unpleasantly make the acquaintance of at least one of them."

From his place on the bench, Frank Monroe watched with a speculative expression as they strolled away. The sly grin he had seen made him wish he had been close enough to eavesdrop on the whole conversation. As they passed from sight in the crowded walkway, he turned his attention to the building they seemed to have been discussing. But having missed lunch at the senior center, he soon lost his curiosity about them in favor of satisfying the emptiness of his stomach.

The Union Jack displayed on the outside wall made him wonder if the place might possibly sell real British bangers.

Most likely not, he decided with a sigh. But they would be likely to have fish and *chips,* as the English called french fries, and hopefully, malt vinegar to splash over them. Whatever he decided to have for lunch, it would go better with a pint of stout. In his youth, Monroe had studied at Oxford, and he fondly remembered pints in pubs with fellow students. Well, he could get something to go and take it to The Sluice Box, a fairground pub not far away, where he could buy a Guinness, possibly even on tap.

The appeal of this idea set him scooting forward on the bench. He enjoyed people-watching as the crowd of so many different kinds of folks swirled around him. He remembered the woman with the dog, who had collided with a youngster in pirate paint a few minutes earlier. He had easily identified her as Jessie Arnold, an Iditarod musher often seen in print. He thought she lived somewhere nearby. There had been something in the paper about her being injured in a plane crash that summer, and he frowned, trying to recall the circumstances without success.

But he had rested long enough, and it was time to explore more of the fair and eat lunch. Getting up, he slung his leather knapsack over a shoulder and set out toward the food booth across the plaza. Swinging the cane he seldom needed as he walked, he wondered again what Doris Richards had done when she had been unable to locate him at the market. Undoubtedly she had caused a ruckus and had everyone frantically searching. Then she would have notified his long-suffering nephew, generating resentment and frustration at another situation with which his nephew would be called upon to deal.

Monroe couldn't help grinning at the idea of a little payback.

A small blond girl in a bright pink jacket smiled in return as she passed, a wad of matching pink cotton candy in one hand, her mother's hand in the other. Her wide eyes reminded Monroe of the daughter and only child he had lost to pneumonia at about the same age. Though Beth's hair had been dark and curly, her eyes had been much the same blue.

Squaring his shoulders, he stepped out smartly in the direction of fish and chips, relishing his freedom of choice before a sip of the anticipated Guinness so much as passed his lips.

•

Were you at the Iditarod booth for the rest of the afternoon, Jessie?" Becker asked.

"Yes—it was pretty busy." She thought back and went on, "By the time I left it was almost dark. I was tired and ready to go home, but when I passed The Sluice Box, I was sucked right in by Hobo Jim's music. Then I met Hank Peterson, so I stayed a while longer." She hesitated and frowned. "I think that was the last thing I really enjoyed at the fair."

It was late when Jessie headed for the vendors' parking lot in the middle of the fairground behind The Sluice Box. Between five and seven o'clock, as people left their day jobs, the adult crowd had increased and a lot of people had stopped by the booth to talk to her, but by eight it had thinned considerably. As she approached The Sluice Box, the fair's largest pub, she realized part of the reason why. Foot-tapping strains of music drifted out through the open double doors, and she recognized the voice and guitar of Alaska's favorite troubadour, Hobo Jim.

The temptation was too much. Nodding to the security guard who waved her through the door, she slipped inside. Tank obediently sat down close to her feet as she stood against the wall to listen and watch for a few minutes.

The Sluice Box was housed in a permanent building, unlike many of the vendors' accommodations, which were built or hauled in temporarily for the run of the fair and removed or dismantled afterward. Vendors registered and were assigned the spaces they occupied and would often find themselves in a different location each year. The Sluice Box, however, remained where it had been constructed of studs and plywood, with a dirt and gravel floor that collected cigarette butts and peanut shells and allowed spilled beer to drain away. Narrow shelves, just wide enough to hold a beer, ran along the walls, which were covered with posters and signs advertising the various kinds of beer for sale at the bar.

Jessie stood in a room the size of a tennis court, so packed with people there was hardly room to breathe, let alone sit down. Lines of thirsty people snaked around to her right, awaiting service at a long counter where several bartenders were dispensing beer into plastic cups and ringing up sales as fast as they could work. To her left were a number of tall, narrow tables for customers who preferred to stand as they drank and enjoyed the music. At the other end of the room were wooden picnic tables with attached benches. These were jammed with folks all paying enthusiastic attention to a stage beyond them where Hobo Jim, with his guitar, was perched on a tall stool. The room rocked to the infectious rhythm of his music, and the crowd clapped and joined in with the song he was singing about the Alaska Railroad. At a nearby table she noticed three men from an ongoing lumberjack show, in red plaid shirts, jeans, and suspenders, all rhythmically waving their beer as they lustily sang along.

"Hey, Jessie," a voice called out as applause for the song began to die away. "Over here."

Searching the faces of those in line for beer, she recognized Hank Peterson's grin of greeting. A good friend, he had helped to build her new cabin earlier that summer, but she hadn't seen him in several weeks.

"Want a beer?" he called over the volume of the crowd.

The sound system cut in before Jessie could reply. She shrugged in defeat. "Yes, please."

Though the sound of her voice was lost, he caught her meaning and nodded. She watched him make it to the bar, where he greeted the bartender, a casual friend whom Jessie knew only by his first name, Eric. He grinned and raised a hand in her direction—a long-distance hello. She waved back, then saw that Hank had stopped at one of the tall tables where a space had opened up. Keeping Tank close, she threaded her way through the crowd of people to join him and found that from there, it was possible to see over the heads of those sitting at the lower tables.

"Thanks," she shouted in Hank's ear, and took a grateful sip of the cool Alaskan Amber he had set down in front of her.

It was too noisy for conversation, for Hobo Jim, as usual,

had the crowd's undivided attention and enthusiasm. Finishing a number, he leaned forward to speak into the microphone.

"Last year," he told the audience, "when we did wolf howls to this next song, they could hear us at the Borealis Theater. This year I want 'em to hear us all the way to the grandstand behind the big barn. Okay?"

The answer was a roar of applause and practice howls, as Hobo Jim launched into the song, accompanied by clapping and foot stomping. At the appropriate time, everyone, including Jessie and Hank, howled along with him, and in the confined space of The Sluice Box, the sound was all but deafening. Even Tank joined in, making Jessie laugh and adding a note of realism to the mix.

"Who's got the wolf in here?" Hobo Jim asked when the noise died down enough for him to be heard. "Is that you, Jessie?" he asked, peering under a hand lifted to shade his eyes from the glare of the overhead spotlight. "Hey, folks—we're in famous company tonight. That's Jessie Arnold, one of our best Iditarod racers. And she's evidently brought along a canine singer. Thanks, Jessie."

Jessie waved him a greeting, and as people turned to look, he launched into what was arguably his most well-known number, "The Iditarod Trail Song," in her honor. In seconds the room rocked with sound as everyone joined in with the familiar words of the chorus: "I did, I did, I did the Iditarod Trail."

Singing made her thirsty, and she soon finished the beer Hank had brought her.

"Ready for another?" he asked, draining his as well.

"Here," she told him, holding out Tank's leash. "Hold him, and I'll get this one."

"Woman after my own heart." Peterson grinned, taking the leash as Jessie made her way through the crowd and joined the line at the bar where her friend Eric was busily drawing beer, keeping customers cheerful with humorous banter as he worked.

She was next in line at the taps when a scuffle broke out in the line next to her.

"Hey, this is a line, fella. Go to the back of it."

She saw that a short blond man in a blue windbreaker was ignoring the others waiting and trying to force his way up to the bar.

"Oh, shit," she heard Eric say in an angry, disgusted tone. "Is he back in here *again*?"

He came out from behind the bar, and approached the offender, looming over him by fully six inches. "Told you not to come back," he growled impatiently, made a handful of the back of blond man's jacket collar, and marched him toward the closest door, in the rear of the pub beyond the bar. With a not-so-gentle shove, he ejected the protesting man, who was trying inefficiently to take a swing at his captor. "Come back and I'll have you arrested." All but dusting off his hands, he came scowling back, but as he regained his place at the taps his expression relaxed into a grin.

"Hey, sorry about that. Some people shouldn't drink, and he's been a problem all night. Eighty-sixed him when he got shit-faced and tried to start a fight with me earlier. What can I do you for?"

It was a side of Eric that Jessie had never seen, but she told herself that it was a demanding job, even without problem customers. Eric was usually as easygoing as anyone she knew, so she excused his behavior as frustration and forgot it as she carried the two beers back to join Hank.

I didn't stay long after that," Jessie told them. "It had been a tiring day, and I was coming back the next morning, so I went home. I started out the front door of The Sluice Box, but there was some kind of commotion—the security guard and another guy yelling at a kid who was riding a bicycle on the walkway. Rather than get involved, I worked my way through the crowd inside and slipped out the back door."

"Did you see anyone in back of the bar?" Phil Becker asked.

Jessie thought for a moment before answering.

"I don't remember anyone except a guy in that small stand of trees—the one with the picnic table. It looked like the one Eric had thrown out a little while earlier. He was sitting on the ground, leaning against a tree. I assumed he was drunk, so I avoided him, found my truck, and went on home."

CHAPTER 6

Becker frowned in thought. "But you didn't go home, did you, Frank?" he asked, turning to Frank Monroe. "Why not?"

The old man shook his head. "No," he said, "I didn't." He shifted position in the overstuffed chair. "I thought it over and found I had no inclination to return to that unlockable room at the center," he said with a shrug of discomfiture. It was quiet for a moment as he considered how to justify his subsequent actions. "I had a debate with myself, you see. We learn guilt early, at our mother's knee, so doing what is expected of us is how we tend to fit into society with the least amount of conflict. But I thought of all the things in my life that I'd done because they were expected of me, and the mental pile of shoulds *and* ought-tos *grew until it was a mountain compared to my* want-tos. Should *and* ought-to *was what got me pigeonholed in that unlockable room in the first place, wasn't it? All at once it seemed insufferable. I'd escaped successfully and made it to the fair. So I decided, for once, to do what* I *wanted. Therefore I didn't go back."*

A grin spread itself across his face as he remembered that small but significant personal rebellion. "And it felt great—better than great. It felt grand!"

As several of those in the room smiled, nodded agreement, and began to break in with questions, he reached into a pocket, extracted a much used and favored pipe, and began to pat his pockets in search of tobacco.

"Here. Try some of this," the other pipe smoker in the group suggested, tossing his own pouch across to land in Monroe's lap.

"Gratefully, thanks." The old man filled his pipe, puffed it alight, and settled back into his chair. "Good stuff."

"What did you do?"

"Where did you sleep?"

"Did you hide?"

Becker overrode the rest. "That was the night you met Danny, wasn't it?"

The man and boy gave each other gleeful, conspiratorial glances that erased the years between them in the enjoyment of being the only two who knew the answers to the flood of questions and more.

"Shall we tell them?"

"I guess."

"First," Monroe began, "I spent the better part of the evening where you were, Jessie—in the pub, listening to Hobo Jim."

"I didn't see you."

"But I saw you *and heard that dog of yours howl." He nodded at Tank, whose head still rested on Danny's knee. "I was sit-*

ting at a table on the east side of the room, but it was pretty crowded."

"Where were you, Danny? Why didn't you go home?" Jessie asked the boy who was petting the dog. "You must have known that your folks would be worried about you."

"Yeah, but I knew my dad would be home by then, and he'd be really steamed at me. I'd locked my bike to a tree in that little park across from the place where fair people camp out in tents."

"Where I saw the guy against the tree."

"Uh-huh, I guess so. After Glen and Tommy left, I went back for the bike, but I sat at the picnic table for a long time, listening to the music in the dark and not wanting to go home and be in trouble. But then . . ."

The fair was bright with thousands of colored lights along the walkways and beckoning from the booths. The midway rides spun bright patterns in the air as they carried shrieking passengers up and around. Most of the younger children had been taken home, and the evening crowd that wandered the grounds was mostly teenagers and adults. Besides Hobo Jim at The Sluice Box, other performers were taking their turns on several outdoor stages, and the centrally located Orion Dome was full to capacity for a group of Chinese acrobats. In a ring at the grandstand, an equestrian show was going on.

Danny Tabor sat in the shadows at a picnic table behind The Sluice Box pub in a small stand of perhaps a dozen trees, feeling less than ten years old, contemplating a long ride home on his bicycle and wondering just how long he would be grounded for this escapade. The pirate makeup he had worn all afternoon was mostly gone or smeared, leaving what looked vaguely like a black eye and the remains of a painted scar on his left cheek. Slowly he pulled the skull and crossbones bandana from his head and untied the knot in it. His backpack lay beside him on the table, and he started to put the bandana inside but changed his mind and tucked it into the back pocket of his jeans instead. Having his friends gone made him feel guilty and out of sorts, unable to forget that he had disobeyed his parents.

Finally he got up slowly and unlocked the chain that held his bicycle to the tree, reluctant but resigned to starting toward home. As he was about to put the chain in his backpack, the rear door of The Sluice Box opened with a crash and a man in a blue jacket came stumbling through it, ejected by someone inside.

". . . have you arrested," Danny heard an angry voice say before the door was slammed shut.

The man who had been pushed out almost fell, but instead caught his balance, swung clumsily around, and gave the door a one-fingered salute. "Asshole!" he yelled, but there was no one to hear or to see the furious look on his face, except for Danny.

For a minute, as the boy watched, he seemed about to go back in, but he apparently reconsidered. Turning away, he headed off along a gravel access road that ran close to the trees and table. Until he disappeared, the boy stood still, not wanting to call attention to himself. When the man was gone, he turned back to put the lock and chain in the backpack.

The bicycle had a carrier over its rear wheel in which he intended to secure his backpack. He had started to reach for it when the sound of approaching voices caused him to freeze again, then step farther back, silent and all but invisible in the dark beneath the trees.

Not far from the pub and across a narrow dirt road, within the semicircle of a small grandstand, was an arena used at regular intervals during daylight hours for a lumberjack show that was sponsored by a local building supply company. There, encouraged by cheering support from a crowd in the bleachers, three or four men experienced in working with logs would compete with each other in a variety of contests. Using their well-developed skills, they raced to be first to cut through logs with an ax or saw or to climb tall poles and chop a section off the top. Balancing in twos on a log that floated in a small pond, they rolled it with their feet in an attempt to make each other lose balance and fall into the water. One of the demonstrations was marksmanship in hurling the heavy, knife-sharp axes at targets painted on the end of a log. But after dark this area was quiet and unused, though people who worked at the fair passed around or through it periodically, heading for their vehicles in a lot next door or to the campground full of tents on the opposite side.

As Danny listened and watched, two men appeared in the arched entrance that divided the bleachers and led into the arena behind them. It was too dark to see either of them clearly under the arch. But as they stepped from it into the dim edges of the light from a fixture over the pub's back door, Danny recognized the man who had been ejected from the pub a few minutes earlier. The other was taller, wore a baseball cap, and was carrying a red gym bag. The shorter, heavier man walked with his hands shoved into the pockets of the blue jacket. He was shaking his head and saying something with which his companion evidently disagreed, for they stopped just outside the arch and faced each other, silhouetted against a light in the nearby parking lot and closer to Danny than to the back door of The Sluice Box. Over the sound of Hobo Jim singing inside the pub, Danny could make out only a few words of what the two were saying, but from their tight, angry voices and posturing, it was evident that they were arguing.

"No, dammit . . . you crazy? . . . n't quit now."

The shorter man shook his head. ". . . on't work . . ."

". . . will, but you gotta . . ."

"I'm out . . . not gonna get . . ."

A clinched fist was shaken. ". . . even think about it, you . . . na bitch. He's not gonna stand for . . ."

"No. I'm out."

The shorter man wheeled to walk away, but before he could leave, the other man grabbed his jacket by the lapel and yanked him back.

"You . . . too much. He's gonna be pis . . ."

Pushing and shoving, they struggled—one to free himself, one to prevent. Then the shorter man threw a punch that rocked his opponent, but not enough to make him let go. There was a break in the music, and Danny heard the sound of fabric ripping.

"Damn you!" The taller man suddenly heaved away the

red bag he had been carrying, in order to free both hands, with which he assaulted the other man in a flurry of blows, driving him to his knees. The bag flew through the air, and something metal clinked inside as it landed against Danny's backpack in the shadows.

The shorter man regained his feet and the battle resumed, but he was taking the brunt of the fight. With one extra-hard punch, the taller man knocked him all but senseless to the ground.

It was time to get out of there, Danny decided. Snatching his backpack from the ground, he gave his bicycle a shove, hopped on, and was already pedaling hard when he heard an angry yell from behind him.

"Hey, kid. Come back here with that."

Glancing down, he discovered that he had grabbed not only his blue backpack but, by one handle, the red bag that had fallen next to it. Not about to go back into the middle of an angry brawl and unable to separate the twisted handles, he swung both bags over a handlebar and pedaled harder, aware of the sound of feet pounding the pavement behind him as the taller man followed at a run.

There weren't many people on the walkway, but there were enough to make it difficult to maintain speed on his bicycle. Swerving between and around them, Danny managed to avoid directly colliding with anyone.

"Hey! Wadda ya think you're doing?" someone shouted. "Watch it."

Another lost equilibrium and sat down hard on the pavement as Danny zipped past a little too close. As the boy pedaled by The Sluice Box, the security guard at the door ran out into his path, spread out his arms in an attempted barrier, and yelled at him, "Stop! You can't ride a bicycle on the grounds." With an instinctive maneuver of the handlebars, Danny swung around him and continued his escape.

A space with no pedestrians opened up on the walkway and gave him an opportunity to glance behind him and see that his pursuer had stopped and, angrily waving an arm in the direction the bicycle had gone, was talking to the security guard. Looking ahead again, he found that he had reached the central plaza, where there was plenty of room to speed up. But where should he go?

In a quick turn to the right, he headed for the nearest gate and had begun to pass the long side of the livestock barn when it occurred to him that the security guards had radios. This meant that the guard at the gate would probably have been notified to be looking for him. This was not appealing. Without his bicycle it might not have been too difficult to find someplace around the fenced perimeter of the fairground to sneak away, but having it made that impossible, and he was not about to leave it behind.

Slowing as he came to the end of the huge barn, he hopped off the bicycle and pushed it into the dark behind the building, hoping no one had seen. Propping the bicycle against the wall in the shadows, he crept back to the corner and peered cautiously around it in the direction he had come. Except for a couple holding hands as they walked away from him toward the southern gate, there was hardly anyone in sight—no security guards, no angry man in a baseball cap, no one threatening.

Taking a deep breath, Danny retreated into the dark and leaned against the wall, thinking hard about what he should do next. If they weren't looking for him now, they very soon would be, and the bicycle was a dead giveaway.

Leaving his wheels where they were, he walked the length of the barn, looking along it for some kind of cover and finding nothing but a few weeds and the back door to the building. The far southeast corner came close to the grandstand where an equestrian show was taking place. He could hear commentary from a loudspeaker system and applause from the people watching the horses being put through their paces in an arena much larger than the one used by the lumberjacks. Near that corner, a wobbly wire and slat fence ran up and was attached to the wall of the barn. Looking closely, he discovered that there was a space between the two that was just large enough to crawl through. Beyond it was a stack of straw in bales. Some of the bales had been broken open and pitched into a pile, and one had fallen and broken open behind the stack.

Quickly Danny returned to his bicycle and wheeled it to the space in the fence where it connected to the barn. It took a few minutes to maneuver it through the narrow space and required tugging at the wire to widen it enough for the handlebars and pedals to fit. But when that was accomplished and the vehicle lay on its side, it was easy to cover it with the straw from the broken bale, concealing it from casual observation.

Without his bicycle, he might be able to escape the fairground undetected. But Danny was decidedly reluctant to leave his treasured mode of transportation behind, and it would be a long walk home. The idea of not having to face his parents held its own appeal, though he didn't want to face the man whose bag he had accidentally snatched up with his backpack either.

Taking both the red bag and his own backpack, he crawled back through the space between the fence and the building and went along the wall to the back door of the barn. Tentatively he tried the knob. It turned. The door was open. With a sigh of relief, he opened it a crack and peeked into the lighted area inside the huge barn.

A few people still wandered among the animal pens where cows, pigs, sheep, and goats, as well as a few llamas and alpacas, were on display. They took up two-thirds of the space to Danny's right, each with a layer of straw for the animal's comfort. Beyond them was an enclosed show ring and beyond that a fenced petting area popular with children during the day to get *up close and personal* with a variety of animals that were rotated in and out. The floor in this section of the barn was dirt, and a wide walkway extended from the back door to the bays at the front. To the left, another door led into another large cement-floored room that housed poultry and rabbits in dozens of smaller raised cages.

Without further thought, Danny slipped in and looked quickly around to see if he had been observed. Almost immediately several of the ceiling lights high overhead suddenly went out, startling him into a step backward that brought him up against the door he had just closed behind him.

"The farm exhibits will be closing in five minutes," a disembodied voice announced from a loudspeaker directly over his head, making him jump again. Then more lights in the rafters abruptly went out.

Someone would soon come to lock the door and make sure the building was empty, Danny thought, frowning. Should he go back out or stay? It would be better to stay, he decided, but how could he avoid being made to leave with the rest of the people who were now heading for the broad front doors? There must be someplace to hide. He looked nervously around the immediate area. There was nothing close to where he stood, but the smaller room might have possibilities.

Without further thought, he stepped to his left, through the door into the rabbit and poultry room, and discovered two tables that had been pushed together, each with a fabric skirt that covered it, top to floor. A glance assured him that the few people still inside were headed for the doors at the far end and no one was looking in his direction. Diving behind the nearest table, he crawled under it, banging one of the bags he carried on a metal leg with a clunk that he hoped no one heard. He sat cross-legged, listening intently to the sounds within the building, none of them close to his hiding place.

For perhaps five minutes there was nothing but the faraway murmur of voices from the other end of the long room. They soon ceased, but the footsteps of a single person passed the table. Danny heard the jingle of keys as the person walked away. Then, abruptly, all the overhead lights went out, leaving him in inky darkness. There was a rustle—some nearby rabbit moving around in its cage—then silence, complete and total.

For a few minutes Danny stayed where he was without moving, feeling very singular and a little frightened in the complete absence of light, and hearing nothing and nobody else. Then, as his eyes adjusted to the dark, he noticed that dim light defined the lower edge of the table skirt. Enough of it leaked in faintly to let him see the underside of the table. Rocking forward onto his knees, intending to peek out in search of its source, he froze in astonishment and alarm as he heard something brush against the fabric skirt that hung between the two tables. Without warning, a hand fell on his shoulder, startling him into an involuntary jerk and yelp. He started to scramble away from the touch and out from under the table. Before he could accomplish it, the hand slid down his arm, tightened its grip, and a low voice whispered eerily close in his ear, "*I wouldn't do that if I were you.*"

CHAPTER 7

"You 'bout scared the pee out of me!" Danny said to Monroe with a grin.

"Danny," his mother remonstrated from her place in a chair by the stove, frowning at his language.

"Sorry," he told her and ducked his head, ears turning pink.

Phil Becker choked on his beer, unable to keep from a guffaw in the middle of a swallow. "It's probably true, you know?" he commented, when he could speak.

"All the same." But as Mrs. Tabor handed him a tissue from her sweater pocket, her lips twitched in amusement.

"I had no intention of alarming you," Monroe assured Danny. "I thought you were about to crawl from under the table, and it was far too soon for safety. You made quite a racket getting under there. I took a quick peek beneath the table cover to see who you were, but I overlooked the fact that you had no idea I was

concealing myself beneath the other table. Sorry I frightened you."

"You?" Jessie sat up with a grin of disbelief. "Under a table? Frank! Really?"

"You may well find the image entertaining," he told her with a lordly lift of his chin. "But my concealment was actually rather well planned. I had decided that I valued my freedom more than my dignity. What is dignity anyway but a facade for others? When you're by yourself it matters very little. Think about the way you behave when you're alone compared to your public persona. Besides, the more you enjoy living freely, the less you need dignity as a shield, because you stop making assumptions about what others may think of you."

"Well, you scared me good, anyway," Danny told him again. "But it's okay. After I found out who you were and why you were hiding, too, I was glad you were there. But I was really *glad—when we almost got caught . . ."*

Hold still, young man," the whisperer instructed as Danny writhed in an attempt to dislodge the hand that gripped his arm. "I don't intend to do you harm. It's not safe out there."

"Let go of me!"

"I will release you when you desist struggling."

The boy quit trying to pull away, but Monroe, feeling that he was still tensed to flee given the opportunity, sustained his hold on the youngster's arm and moved into the space under the boy's table.

"There's a barn manager wandering around out there

somewhere," he whispered in warning. "You may unexpectedly encounter him if you abandon this shelter. And if you aren't quiet he will discover us both. Understand?"

He felt the tension leave the boy's body as he nodded his acceptance of the idea. Slowly Monroe relaxed his grip and released the boy, who turned around and sat cross-legged to study his unanticipated companion.

"Who are you?" Danny demanded, matching his whisper to that of his captor.

"No one who will hurt you or reveal your secret," Monroe returned. "My name is Frank Monroe, and I'm just a senior citizen playing hooky from an unpleasant situation at the moment, as, from the evidence, I suspect are you. Now, do *you* have a name?"

Eyes now fully adjusted to the dim light filtering under the table from the room outside, the boy was able to make out the elderly face of the man who had grabbed and then released him.

He's a really old guy, Danny thought in surprise, and wondered why a senior citizen was hiding under a table. But the man smiled encouragingly at him, waiting for an answer to his question.

"Danny. My name's Danny."

"All right, good. Now we have the foundation for an alliance."

"Alliance?"

No one Danny knew talked like this. *Who is this guy?* he wondered—*and what does* alliance *mean? Maybe I should find another place to hide.*

"Association—coalition—confederacy, if you will. As it is obvious that neither of us wishes to be detected, we'll be better off if we join forces and cooperate. Right?"

"I guess so," Danny agreed hesitantly, not at all sure about the big words this man was using or that they would be better off *joining forces*. This guy *was* a grown-up, after all, and grown-ups usually stuck together. Sometimes they told you one thing, then let you down by *doing* another. "You won't tell that barn manager I'm here?"

Monroe shook his head. "And have him discover me, too? I'm not under here for my health, you know. No, I won't tell if you won't."

Danny cocked his head and stared at the old man, considering the risk of trusting him. He couldn't think of a reason that anyone would crawl under a table if he didn't want to hide, as this odd person said he did. For the moment, at least, it seemed to be okay. *I can always lose him later,* he decided, and finally agreed.

"I won't. I promise."

"Good again. Now, what are you hiding from, young man?"

"What are *you* hiding from?" Danny demanded. "You first."

So, thought Monroe, with a smile he didn't allow to reach his mouth, *the boy has spirit.* The youngster's spunk pleased him. He nodded and explained briefly that he didn't like the place he lived and had decided to stay at the fair.

"But, as everyone is required to leave at closing time and I had nowhere to go, I decided to find myself an invisible place to spend the night. This was the best of several alternatives. Now, why are you under here?"

Danny explained that, along with his backpack, he had accidentally grabbed a bag that belonged to someone else and that that someone was chasing him.

"Why didn't you give it back?"

"He was really mad—he'd been hitting the other guy. I thought he might hit *me*."

"What *other guy*?" Monroe asked, now paying close attention.

The whole story came tumbling out—the fight Danny had witnessed between the two men, how he had pedaled away from it and hidden his bicycle, come into the barn through the back door, and found the space under the table.

"Why didn't you just go home?" Monroe questioned and waited, guessing some of the answer from the way Danny refused to meet his eyes and looked down in uneasy silence for a long moment. It was very late for someone this boy's age to be out alone.

"Do your parents know where you are?"

Danny's shrug was more of an attempt to distance himself from the subject than an indication that he didn't know. He looked up, took a deep breath, and was about to tell the truth about how he had left home without permission to spend the day at the fair with his two friends. But the sudden sound of voices at the other end of the building caught the attention of both man and boy—voices that grew louder, accompanied by the footsteps of two people headed in their direction. Disturbed by the sounds, an irritated goose honked in annoyance and another answered. A peacock joined in with its distinctive screech. Ignoring the birds, the two people walked closer.

"Sh-h-h," Monroe warned softly. Danny nodded, and they both sat very still to listen without moving.

"You're sure you didn't see a kid with a bicycle?" asked one of the invisible men.

"Very sure. Wouldn't have let him bring it in here. Anyway, everyone's gone now. You can see the barn's empty."

The footsteps passed in front of the two skirted tables, inches from where Danny and Frank Monroe sat still as mice, both holding their breath. A rabbit, agitated by the passing of the two men, rattled the feeding tray in its cage as it moved.

"What was that?"

"Just a rabbit—jumpy as you are."

"I want that kid. He stole my camera bag."

They moved on through the door between the two rooms of the barn, and there was the sound of the back door thumping shut after one of them opened it for some reason.

"Don't you lock this?"

"No. The security guys need it to check on the place after I leave."

"How long will you be here?"

"Another hour or so. Got some cleaning up to do in the petting zoo. But no kid, bicycle or not, will come in here with the doors shut."

"Well, he didn't go out through any of the gates, so he must still be on the grounds somewhere. Keep an eye out, and call me if you spot him."

From under the table, Danny and Frank heard the summons of a cell phone ringing.

One of the men answered it.

"Yeah."

A pause.

"Sorry. There's been a couple of setbacks."

Another pause.

"Look. Some kid stole my bag with the camera and stuff. I've been scouring the grounds, trying to find the little shit."

A significantly longer pause.

"I know. I *won't*. Look, I can't talk now, and I've got a problem with Curt to take care of. Yes—Curt. I'll take care of it."

Pause.

"I *said* I'd take care of it. Just let me find that kid and I'll get back to you."

He hung up, and the footsteps faded as the two men moved back toward the front of the barn.

They walked right past and didn't look under the table?"

"Yes," Monroe said, and Danny nodded agreement.

"So you stayed there—all night?"

"It seemed a good idea, as they had already decided the barn was lacking Danny's presence. They didn't know about mine, of course."

"True."

"After the manager left, we took advantage of there being no one to see and moved some straw under the table from the other part of the barn. It made a comfortable enough bed. We were care-

ful not to move and make it rustle when a security guard came through on his rounds a couple of times during the night."

"Didn't you get hungry or thirsty?" Jessie asked.

"I had a bottle of water and, of course, my purloined supplies from the grocery. We made a snack of Vienna sausages on crackers and the oranges before we took a nap."

"Like a picnic," Danny chimed in. "It was fun."

"What about the red gym bag?" Jessie asked. "Wasn't that when you found out what was in it?"

As the two satisfied their hunger, Monroe thought about the comment made by the unseen person who had passed the table without knowledge of their presence. *I want that kid. He stole my camera bag.* Swallowing the Vienna sausage he was chewing, he turned to the boy.

"Have you looked inside that extra bag you're carrying?"

Danny shook his head. "I thought I'd just leave it somewhere, so somebody would find it and turn it in."

Monroe thought for long enough to peel an orange.

"They might not turn it in, you know. Perhaps it would be more advisable to see just what it contains before determining a course of action concerning it. Yes?"

"Okay." Danny reached for the red bag and handed it to Monroe. "Here. You look." But he leaned forward to see as the man unzipped the bag and opened it.

Though it was dim under the table, there was enough light to see what was inside as he lifted out a 35mm camera complete with flash attachment. Feeling around in the bag, he identified several rolls of film, four of which had been used—if lack of the strip of film that pulls it into the camera was an indication. There were also several photographs of the fairground.

"No wonder the owner's concerned about it," he said, turning the camera around so he could read Minolta on the front. "This is a valuable item you've accidentally acquired, Danny. Not one you'd want to leave lying around just anywhere for some less scrupulous person to liberate."

He looked up to see that the boy was staring wide-eyed at the camera, his face a study in desperation. "I didn't steal it. Honest. I didn't mean to take it at all. It just happened."

Monroe laid a hand on his arm in consolation. "It's all right, young man. I believe you. We must simply think of a way to get it back to the owner in the morning. I think perhaps there's accommodation for lost items at the security office, don't you? I'll take it, if you like."

But Danny declined the offer.

"No. I'll do it. I took it, after all, whether I meant to or not. I should make sure he gets it back, I guess."

"Good lad." That the boy would take responsibility for his own mistakes pleased the old man enormously. "We'll see about it tomorrow then."

So you stayed there that night," Becker commented.

"And woke up early, expecting to do the right thing with the camera equipment and film."

"What about you, Jessie? You came back the next morning to a much different fair, right?"

[illegible]

[illegible] That the boys [illegible] responsible for [illegible] the old man [illegible]

[illegible]

CHAPTER 8

Right," Jessie agreed. "It turned into a total nightmare." She stretched forward to lay a hand on Tank's head. "We came back to the fair, and I started to the Iditarod booth. But at the entrance to the lumberjack arena there was a bunch of people standing around: security guards, police, state troopers, and others who had just stopped to see what was going on. You were there, Phil—one of the only people I knew. I stopped for a minute to see what was going on and heard somebody say they'd found a dead man in the pond."

When Jessie arrived at ten that morning it was bright with sunshine, but behind the mountains of the Chugach range to the east, a gray bank of cloud hinted at the possibility of rain later in the day. The air coming in through the open window of the pickup smelled warm and fresh, but she assessed the clouds as she drove the few miles between her house and the fair and was glad she had thought to bring a waterproof jacket. It was the sort of weather she called "push-me-pull-you," the kind it was impossible to accurately predict. The threat of rain would most likely cut down the number of people at the fair, especially since there was a week and a half before it closed, and visitors would assume they could visit on a better day.

Flashing her pass and a smile at the gate guard, she drove through to the employee parking lot, where she took one of the last spaces available. Vendors and fair personnel clearly weren't staying away.

Locking the pickup, she started across the lot with Tank on his leash, intending to go through the passageway beside The Sluice Box. She was startled to find the end of it closest to the lumberjack arena crowded with people, most of them fair workers on their way to their jobs. Their attention was focused on several law enforcement officers and security people inside the arena. Beyond them, at the arena's entrance, a state trooper's patrol car was parked, along with what she recognized as the van used by the Anchorage crime lab, which was responsible for forensics statewide. As she approached, a man she knew turned and started toward the pub—the bartender from the evening before.

"Eric," she called, and he stopped to wait for her to reach him. "What's going on?"

"Nasty. About an hour ago someone found a dead man floating in the logrolling pond."

"Who is it?"

He frowned and shook his head. "Don't know."

"What happened?"

"Don't know that either. Maybe he fell in and drowned."

"But that pond is only hip deep. I watched that show last year."

"Well, maybe he had a snoot full." The bartender shrugged, helpless to supply information.

Jessie's memory took her back to the night before and the man she had glimpsed sitting under one of the trees. Could it be the same person? Could he have been so drunk that he staggered into the pond by accident? Maybe. An accidental death would explain the presence of the crime lab van.

"I saw someone that I thought might have had a few too many last night as I was leaving. But he was in the trees by the picnic table."

"Oh yeah?" His eyes widened in interest. "Maybe you better tell one of the troopers or PPD officers. I don't really know anything except that we try to cut people off before they have too many. But with Hobo Jim on stage last night, it was a madhouse and we might not have noticed—especially if someone else was buying his beer." Shifting his feet, he started to move toward the pub again. "Sorry, Jessie, but I've got to get inside. We're about to open, and there're still a few kegs to replace in the cold room."

She waved him away. "That's fine. You go. I'll find someone to tell, though it's probably not the same guy."

"Stay well," Eric told her as he moved away and went into The Sluice Box through the back door.

As Jessie turned back toward the entrance to the arena, a

tall slim trooper whom she recognized, partly by his western hat, stepped up, raised a hand for quiet, and addressed the gathering, which was growing by the minute. Now, just after opening time, it included a few early fair goers.

"Listen, folks. We've got a possible crime scene here, and it won't help us to have all of you milling around. Please go on about your business and let us do ours."

The people obliged, if slowly and with a low, speculative murmur. They began to move through the passage next to the pub, toward the center of the fairground, many casting frowns or curious looks over their shoulders. Jessie stood where she was and was soon rewarded by a quick smile from Phil Becker, as he saw and acknowledged her. But a look of concern immediately replaced his warm greeting.

"Hey, Jessie."

She walked to where he stood, and he knelt to give Tank a pat or two.

"Phil, I don't know what you've got in there, but I thought you should know that I saw a guy sitting under one of the trees last night as I left to go home. He looked asleep or passed out, and might have been drunk enough to wander in there and drown."

Becker stood up frowning, his attention immediately focused on what she was saying. "Tell me about it. What time was it? What can you remember about the guy you saw? What was he wearing, for instance?"

"That's all, really. It was between nine-thirty and ten o'clock. He was sitting in the shadow under that tree," she said as she turned and pointed to it. "He was just a silhouette against the little bit of light that came through from beyond, so it was too dark to see colors or what he looked like. The only thing I could see in the light from the back door of the pub was that he had on boots—brown leather boots."

Becker nodded. "That works. This guy does have on similar boots. You came out that back door?"

"Yeah. There was some kind of ruckus going on out front, and with people crowding to get in, it was almost impassable, so I went through the pub and took the back way to the parking lot."

"That lot's for fair workers. You on that list, Jessie?"

"Helping out at the Iditarod booth."

"Should have guessed." Becker grinned. "How's your bad knee?"

"Better, but no racing this winter."

He scowled again in thought, then shook his head. "Since you can't identify the guy you saw, I'd guess there's no way of knowing if it's this one in the pond. But I'll keep it in mind."

As he hesitated to say more, there was a flurry of movement at the logrolling pond, where four officers had waded into the water to retrieve the body. "God dammit!" one of them cursed in a shocked voice. Both Jessie and Becker turned to see that they had lifted and were holding the body facedown at the surface of the water.

"Shit!" Becker swore. "No wonder his feet were all that was visible. That thing was weight enough to hold the rest of him under. There's no way this one drowned."

Even from a distance of forty feet it was possible to see

the ax that was deeply embedded in the back of the dead man's skull.

Jessie gasped and raised a hand to her mouth. One of the fair security guards made a hasty exit through the arena entrance to lose her breakfast in the weeds behind The Sluice Box.

"Get a cover on it," one of the troopers demanded, and a Palmer policeman stepped forward with a piece of blue plastic tarp as the four in the water lifted the body out of the pond.

"Sorry, Jessie," Becker said, already moving away from her. "I'll get back to you if we need more."

"Sure," she told his retreating back. "You know where I'll be."

As the group of law enforcement people shifted to allow the body to be laid on a waiting stretcher, she saw John Timmons, assistant coroner from the crime lab, roll up in his wheelchair and lean to lift the makeshift plastic from what was now his responsibility. She caught the sound of his gravel voice as he snapped an instruction to one of his two assistants, but she couldn't make out what he had said.

Timmons was a good friend and almost a legend in the forensics world. Paralyzed from the waist down by a skiing accident, he hurled himself at his work the same way he hurled himself at everything else in his life—and expected the same from his crew. *This would be no different,* Jessie thought as she turned to make her way to her duties of the day.

Well, it's none of my business this time, she told herself with relief.

CHAPTER 9

Little did you know." Timmons made his first comment of the evening from a place near Frank Monroe where he had parked his wheelchair and had been listening to the recital of past events. "That was just the start of things for you, wasn't it, Jessie?"

"It certainly was, and it got nothing but worse from there," Jessie told them. "I didn't hang around—went straight to the Iditarod booth—so I didn't know any more until later. But it was such an appalling way for someone to die that I couldn't get it out of my mind."

"It was that," Timmons agreed. "But the single blow with the ax at least made his death instantaneous. It's pretty amazing what people will do to each other given rage, fear, or greed. When I did the postmortem that afternoon, though, it was obvious that the victim had been beaten pretty badly before he

was killed, so I guessed it must have involved some combination of those three. Turns out I was pretty close, too, wasn't I, guys?" He grinned at Phil Becker, then across at his partner, another state trooper who sat on the other side of Jessie smoking a briar pipe filled with a fragrant tobacco blend and lighted with a kitchen match.

"You were very close, John," the pipe smoker acknowledged with a grin. "But then, you usually are."

"Exactly who was the dead man?" Doug Tabor, Danny's father, asked Timmons. "I never found out anything but his name."

"We ran prints and found him on file as Curtis Belmont, a small-time thief and hoodlum who had served a couple of years for appropriating a vehicle that didn't belong to him and using it in a convenience store holdup. At that point we had no idea who had killed him, or why."

"I recognized him," Frank Monroe said, suddenly remembering.

"You'd seen him before?"

"The day before. He was the shorter of the two men I had observed in the plaza."

"How did you happen to be in the lumberjack arena that morning?" Becker asked. "Weren't you in the barn?"

"Well, you see, Danny and I had slipped from the barn early, when people started appearing to take care of their animals at seven that morning. Someone would eventually show up to answer questions and hand out printed information at those tables, so I thought it prudent to eradicate the evidence of our occupancy beneath. Putting their feet in a bed of straw might have startled that someone enough to make inquiries. I thought it just possible that we might require that refuge again, and it is

never advisable to burn your bridges. We spent the time, until the fair opened at ten o'clock, in concealment next to Danny's bicycle, behind the straw pile about which he has already informed you. When people began to come in through the southern gate, we joined them, inclined toward finding ourselves some breakfast."

Monroe did not seem to notice that several of those listening to his account could not keep from smiling at his exaggerated choice of words. Young Danny seemed about to question the meaning of several of the largest ones, but shrugged and chimed in with "I was really *hungry."*

"You're always hungry," his mother admonished him. "Hush now, and let Mr. Monroe tell this."

"I was hungry, too." Monroe smiled at the boy. "Danny recalled a vendor who sold a pastry confection he called 'elephant ears.' So I took charge of the two bags he was carrying and enjoined him to purchase these items for both of us while I kept a rather urgent appointment with the gentlemen's facilities near The Sluice Box. After breakfast we intended to convey the red bag with the camera equipment to the lost and found at the security cabin in the middle of the grounds. When I completed my errand Danny had not yet returned and the crowd at the small arena caught my attention. I strolled over to see what was happening and recognized the deceased, but I had no concept of his villainous past, of course."

"And you, Danny?" Timmons questioned. "Did you see the dead man?"

"I stopped to pet Tank after I got us breakfast," Danny said and laid a hand on the dog's head as Jessie nodded agreement.

"So I didn't see that *man. But I saw the* other *one. And* he *saw* me!"

While he stood in line to buy the elephant ears, Danny saw Jessie arrive with her dog and noticed that he was next door to the Iditarod booth. He had, without success, begged his parents for a dog of his own for months and, remembering the woman and her husky from their encounter the day before, decided to take another look at this dog before returning to find Monroe.

"Hi," he said, finding Jessie folding sweatshirts into neat piles behind the counter, Tank sitting at her feet. "Can I pet your dog?"

"Sure." She was impressed at his request for permission. Most kids either went straight to pet a dog or hung back in fear and refused to go near one. It always made her wonder about their past experiences with animals. The tendency people seemed to have lately to train aggressive guard dogs, then exhibit astonishment when they attacked children or adults, always dismayed her and others in the sled dog racing world.

"He likes kids," she told the boy, who immediately went to his knees beside Tank and patted him gently on the head. "Scratch his back and ears," she suggested. "He loves that."

Tank gave Danny a sloppy wet lick on the cheek, making him giggle and hug the dog's neck briefly before he returned to petting him.

"What's his name?"

"Tank. He's the lead dog in my racing team."

"You've been all the way to Nome on your sled, haven't you?" Danny asked, looking up with shining eyes and giggling when Tank gave him another affectionate lick. "That must've been really hard. Didn't you get cold?"

Jessie stopped what she was doing and came across to sit down in a chair next to the boy.

"Yes, I've run the Iditarod several times. And sometimes I was cold. But if you have good equipment, wear the right clothes, and have a warm sleeping bag, you're okay."

"Wow! I'd like to do that someday."

"Maybe you will, if you want to enough."

"I wish I had a dog," Danny said with longing in his voice.

"Ask your parents. Maybe they'll get you one."

"Naw." He shook his head sadly. "I've asked and asked, but Mom always says I'll forget to take care of it."

"Will you?"

He shrugged, a little uncomfortable at the thought. "I don't think so. But sometimes I get busy and forget my chores—like mowing the lawn." He was frowning now and kept his gaze on Tank, refusing to look at Jessie.

"Maybe if you tried hard to be responsible and were careful to remember to do your chores for a long time, they'd see that you could be trusted to care for a dog."

"Maybe," he agreed and finally looked up to meet her eyes.

"Sometimes I forgot when I was your age," Jessie told him, feeling he needed some encouragement. "All kids do. But you get over it, mostly. Once in a while even now I forget things, but *never* my dogs. They depend on me, as your dog would depend on you. They're even more important than the lawn. How would you like it if your mom forgot to give you dinner?"

Danny stopped petting Tank and looked up at her, astonished at her admission that she forgot things, too. He grinned a happier lopsided sort of grin and sat up straight.

"I'll try," he told her. "Try really hard."

"You do that." She smiled back.

Tank, catching the appealing smell of warm pastry in the plastic bag Danny had laid on the floor, nosed at it curiously.

"Can I give him some?" Danny asked, once again pleasing Jessie by asking. She usually didn't feed her dogs sweets, but decided to make an exception considering the boy's polite request.

"Maybe just one bite," she agreed. "What's your name?"

"Danny," he told her, breaking off a rather large bite, which Tank accepted with his usual dignity and swallowed in a gulp.

"I saw you yesterday, didn't I?" Jessie asked, remembering her collision with the pirate in the plaza. "We ran into each other."

Danny grinned. "Yeah, we did."

"But your face paint is gone."

He nodded. "I washed it off."

"So you're back again today?"

"No—well, yes," he stammered and ducked his head, then gave Tank a last pat and got to his feet. "I've gotta go," he said. "My friend is waiting for breakfast."

"That's breakfast?"

His confusing behavior startled Jessie, and she began to ask him another question. But he was already headed for the front of the booth, where the folding doors were spread wide to allow visitors easy access. Just before he disappeared, he turned and asked a quick question.

"Can I come back and see Tank later? He's a really great dog. I'd like one just like him."

She nodded and smiled. "Of course. We'll be here until late this afternoon at least."

He was gone in a flash, leaving Jessie to wonder a little about his odd response to her question. But a Canadian musher she had met during the Yukon Quest, a distance race from Whitehorse to Fairbanks, stepped into the booth, and she forgot about the boy for the moment in greeting him.

Danny, on the other hand, stepped quickly out of the booth on his way to find Frank Monroe. Knowing that by now his new friend was probably wondering what was taking so long, he was inclined to jog through the growing crowd that was now flooding onto the grounds. Disoriented for a moment, he made a left instead of a right turn, realized his mistake, and was about to reverse direction when he all but crashed into someone standing solidly in his way.

Looking up, he was shocked and horrified to see that he had dashed head-on into the owner of the red bag, the man who had chased him the night before. Startled speechless at the boy's sudden appearance, the man loomed over him, a tall and scowling threat in a black T-shirt and baseball cap, his eyes invisible behind reflective sunglasses. For a moment they stared at each other, before the man lunged at Danny, who dodged, spun around, and ran from him.

"Hey! Come back here, kid."

Danny could hear feet pounding behind him, but he had the advantage of his smaller size in disappearing into the crowd that almost an hour after opening thronged the walkway. Panicked, hearing the man yelling behind him, he tore through narrow spaces between people, bumped a few, knocked one woman down, and leaped over a stroller parked in his way. He made an abrupt left turn between two booths, hopped over lines attached to pegs that held up a tent, and crawled frantically into the empty space below a portable cabin that had been hauled in and set on cement blocks for a leather vendor. There he lay hugging the ground, panting and terrified, looking back the way he had come. He expected to see his pursuer appear at any second but hoped he would not.

His heart sank when the man came into sight between the two booths and paused, clearly not sure which way the boy had gone. He looked quickly around, then grabbed a passing woman by the arm with a clear demand for information. Shaking him off in irritation, she waved a hand in Danny's direction and disappeared from sight as she resumed her stroll along the walkway. Seeing the man come hurrying toward him between the two booths he had passed moments earlier, Danny scuttled farther back into the shadows beneath the cabin and held his breath.

Jumping easily over the tent lines and pegs, the man approached until only his feet were visible as he passed the boy's hiding place and went out into a walkway parallel to the one he had just left. There he stopped and stood for a moment, taking the time to look around in all directions. Hoping he would go away, Danny lay very still and quiet. Then he heard footsteps on the stairs that led up into the cabin over his head and voices from above, though he couldn't tell what was being said. In a few seconds, there were more footsteps on the stairs, and looking in that direction, Danny watched the feet of two people go down them and onto the walkway. They stood for a minute before slowly walking away together in the direction of the plaza—Danny's pursuer and a man Danny had noticed before because his hair and beard were dyed a rainbow of colors and stood out from his head in spikes.

When they were gone, Danny laid his forehead on his hands and sighed in relief, still gulping air from exertion and fear. He wished he had not left the red bag and camera with Frank Monroe, for if he had been carrying it, he could have dropped it as he ran, giving the man what he wanted and himself a chance to escape. Now the guy would continue to search the fairground for it. *And me!* Danny thought in discouragement. *Now he knows I'm still here, and so does that other guy with the rainbow hair.*

Slowly, carefully, he crawled from the shelter of the cabin that advertised rocks and fossils for sale. Peering cautiously up and down the walkway before stepping out in the opposite direction from the man who had chased him, he hurried toward the men's rest room, where he expected to find Frank Monroe.

From the door of a booth selling leather items, the thin man with a wild spiked hairdo, each spike dyed a different color, gave him a smile and a wave as he trotted away.

CHAPTER 10

It must have been scary to be chased again. Did you find Mr. Monroe?" Jessie asked him, coming back from the kitchen, where she had gone to get him another can of soda. Handing it over, she resumed her seat on the sofa.

"Yeah," Danny told her, squirming around so he could look up at her as he answered. "He was there waiting for me, and I told him about seeing the guy."

"I knew something was amiss when he came rushing up out of breath and remarkably dusty from hiding on the ground under that cabin," Monroe affirmed. "When he came back, I sent him off to clean up a bit, and then we found a bench on which to sit down and eat our breakfast. Danny caught his breath and related his encounter with the owner of the camera equipment. Upon hearing this, I decided that no time should be wasted in turning that bag in to the lost and found—and ourselves to whoever was looking.

But with the angry owner of the bag lurking about, I had grave misgivings about Danny turning it in alone, as he had planned to do, so we started in that direction together."

The fair's walkways were rapidly filling with people taking advantage of the warm sunny day as Danny and Frank Monroe walked the short distance from the exhibit hall to the security office. Coming around a bend to a point where they could see the building three booths ahead of them, Danny, who was now carrying the red bag, suddenly stopped short and stepped quickly behind Monroe.

"There he is," the boy gasped.

"Where?" Monroe assessed the crowd, searching for a man of the description his young friend had given him.

"Right there in front of the office, talking to that other guy."

When Monroe still couldn't locate the person he meant, Danny pointed as he tugged urgently at the old man's coat sleeve. "There. Right there. Let's get outta here before he sees me."

As he finally identified the man who had made the boy so frantic, Monroe frowned and shook his head. "That can't be him, Danny. They are both security guards."

They were. Both men wore the easily recognizable black T-shirts with SECURITY printed in large white letters across the front. As Monroe stared in their direction, startled and disbelieving, the taller of the two angrily pounded a fist into the palm of his other hand and turned and headed in their direction.

"Oh, shit. I think he saw me," Danny breathed.

"Stay back," Monroe instructed, though it was unnecessary, as the boy was standing so close behind him that he might have been a shadow.

As the guard came closer, Monroe recognized him as the second of the two he had seen in the plaza and recalled that this man's companion had turned up dead in the pond. Instinctively he felt there was something not right about the equation, but had no time to puzzle it through.

Making a quick right turn, Monroe walked them both into the tent of the nearest vendor. It was full of hundreds of T-shirts hanging on racks so near each other that the aisle space between left very little room to move.

"Now," he told the boy, "crawl under this rack, make yourself small, and be silent."

Danny disappeared instantly as Monroe grabbed a green shirt with a colorful gecko printed on the front and turned toward the door through which they had entered. Pretending that he was examining it speculatively with an eye toward purchase, he actually kept a close watch on the walkway outside. He was rewarded when the man Danny had identified passed by and disappeared with only a quick glance at the interior of the booth.

"May I help you?" a female voice suddenly inquired.

Monroe flinched before turning to respond to the clerk, who had quietly come up from behind and startled him. Hanging the shirt carefully back on the rack, he smiled and demurred, tipping his hat as he refused her offer. Off she went to help another customer. Stepping to the front of the booth, he took a long look outside, then called to Danny in a low voice, "Come on out. He's gone."

"Are you *sure!*"

But when he looked again, he noticed that the guard the boy's pursuer had been talking to was *not* gone. Standing in front of the security office, he was intently searching the crowd as it passed, clearly looking for someone.

What, wondered Monroe, *was the best thing to do now? Go ahead to the security office, or avoid it until later, when this man was not standing guard?* Glancing down at Danny, who peered out, pale and frightened, ready to dive back into concealment, he made an uneasy decision he hoped would not be the basis for later regret.

"Come on," he told the boy. "For the moment, we'll let things settle down. Later *I'll* take the bag to the lost and found. Okay?"

Danny nodded. "Thanks," he said and glancing around fearfully, followed his protector out of the booth. "Where'll we go?"

"To that space in the straw behind the big barn, I think," Monroe said, cutting between booths to gain access to a walkway on which they would not be forced to pass the security office. "This is no time to search out another sanctuary."

To save time, they cut straight through rather than going around the barn, which was now full of people wandering through to look at the animals. Many stood in a long line, awaiting a turn for their children in the petting zoo. As the two passed a group of colorful scarecrows leaning against a wall, Monroe hesitated. The contest to make the straw-stuffed figures was evidently over and had been judged, for first, second, and third place ribbons adorned three of them. Beside them on a bale of hay lay a few items of secondhand clothing, leftovers from their creation. Without stopping to examine these, he scooped them up, tucked them under one arm, and continued toward the rear door.

"Wadda ya want those for?" Danny asked.

"You'll see."

When they had made it to the relatively safe place and were out of sight behind the straw bales, Danny threw himself down beside his hidden bicycle and panted in relief.

"I think maybe I should go home," he told Monroe.

The man shook his head.

"I think for the time being you'll be better off right here. Wheeling that bicycle would make you an obvious target for recognition."

While the boy watched curiously, the man sorted through the shirts and pants he had seized from beside the scarecrows and shook out a pair of jeans and a red plaid shirt. "Here. Try these on."

"Why?"

"He's had a good look at you and will be searching for someone wearing your attire. With these as a disguise, you won't be so easy to identify and can join that row of scarecrows."

Danny grinned and pulled the jeans on over his own. They were a couple of sizes too large, so he rolled them up into wide cuffs and used a piece of baling wire as a makeshift belt. Monroe assisted in rolling up the shirtsleeves to the wrists, then assessed the rather amusing result.

"Yes, I think that is quite different and acceptable."

"Do I look like a scarecrow?" Danny giggled.

As Monroe nodded his approval, there was the sudden sound of two men's voices on the other side of the pile of straw bales.

"You take that end and we'll carry it between us."

"Norm said he wanted two."

"They're awkward and heavy. We'll come back for the other one."

There was a rustle and a thump, and the stack was abruptly lowered by one bale.

One of the men grunted. "Oof! You're right. Heavier than I expected."

Danny leaned to peek around one end of the pile to see the two headed away toward the grandstand, the bale of straw carried between them by the wires that held it together.

"Come back here, young man," Monroe demanded with some urgency, giving the tail of the plaid shirt a yank with gnarled fingers. "They'll be right back, and we'd better absent ourselves from the vicinity, at least temporarily."

Danny stumbled back and sat down heavily in the scattered straw.

"What if they find my bicycle?"

"It is more natural to remove bales from the front of the pile. They won't even come close. Come now. We will stroll about among others inside the barn for the time being. But first, tuck that red bag into the space between those two lower bales and cover it with loose straw."

The boy complied, and within seconds the two of them had reentered the barn and made themselves a part of the crowd of fair goers. As they passed the doorway of the room with the rabbits, Monroe glanced inside to see two women seated behind the tables under which he and Danny had spent the previous night. They were chatting together, one occupied in knitting something yellow and blue, and he was glad to have taken the time to clear away the evidence of their overnight residence. He smiled a bit ruefully to himself as he and Danny approached a pen containing two sheep, remembering his stiffness that morning after a night on the straw-covered concrete floor. *Goes with the territory,* he told himself, realizing just how much his sense of freedom overcame any real concern for the physical aches and pains of his age.

Danny dropped to his knees beside the pen and reached through the metal bars with one hand to feel the fleece that some 4-H youngster had obviously carefully washed clean before bringing the animal to be judged. In a moment he was back on his feet and moving along to the neighboring pen, where two lethargic llamas rested in their bed of straw, meditatively chewing their cud, legs tucked neatly under them. This time Danny could barely reach the flank of one of them with the tips of his fingers, but he accomplished the seemingly impossible by stretching his arm to the limit the bars would allow.

"These are softer than the sheep," he told his older friend, glancing up with a pleased expression and reaching again as the llama shifted to a position that was a little closer to the bars of the pen.

Still in a thoughtful mood, Frank Monroe stood leaning on the cane he had been using most of the day to alleviate a dull ache in his left knee. He appraised the people who milled about, noticing that many of them had children in tow or in strollers. As he watched, a father lifted a small boy of perhaps three years old so he could look down at a sow and her piglets in a nearby pen.

As a child, Monroe had lived on a farm in Ohio, where pigs, cows, chickens, and other animals were all a part of his environment. It seemed that fewer farms these days meant that fewer children were acquainted with farm animals. What had been common to him was slowly becoming as exotic to them as animals in a zoo. Currently, most domestic animals were closely confined and raised commercially in huge co-operatives for their meat, milk, and eggs. Even small farmers often possessed more machinery to work their fields than animals for their families—a few chickens, a cow or two, perhaps a pig. The idea made him sad.

But he couldn't help smiling at the giggles of the little boy, who was now reaching to touch the snout of one small piglet that had trotted up to the bars of the pen. The adventurous porker squealed and retreated to its mother, who was lying on her side to feed her brood and who reacted to its shrill complaint with only the unconcerned twitch of an ear.

Straightening his shoulders to relieve another slight ache from his night on the floor, Monroe allowed his gaze to sweep the huge interior of the barn, coming to rest at last on the people coming in through large bays at the front. Just inside, the line for the petting zoo was longer than it had been when they passed it earlier, and the space within the fence was crowded with children and a number of animals that were not too large to frighten or injure them. As he watched, however, two men shoved through the line and headed into the barn, catching his attention. Both wore security black and intently examined the people they pushed aside and passed.

"*Danny,*" he said softly in warning and laid a hand on the boy's shoulder.

"What?"

Alarmed at his tone, the boy tried to stand up, but Monroe increased the pressure of his hand, keeping Danny on his knees. "No—don't move, just listen."

The boy grew still, but tensed to spring, he waited.

"The man who chased you has just come in with another security guard, and they are searching, I would guess, for you."

Another wiggle from Danny.

"I said listen. I want you to do exactly as I say. Remember that they won't recognize you immediately in different clothes, if at all. Now—when I tell you, get up and stand behind me. We're going to walk across the open space behind us to that display of scarecrows along the wall. When we get there and I give you the word, you are to take the hat off the head of that one in the green shirt. Put the hat on and pull it down so it covers most of your face. Then you must sit down next to the one that's propped on the bale of straw. Okay?"

"Okay."

"Whatever happens when they come this way, I want you to stay very still, as if you were a real scarecrow. Can you do that?"

"Yes, but won't they . . . ?"

"Not if you do nothing to attract their attention. The timing of a distraction is my job. You just do yours. They're walking around the petting zoo and looking the other way now. Come quickly."

It worked perfectly. The man walked the boy across to the wall. Hat appropriated and on his head, the boy slipped in to sit as directed. The man walked away casually, leaving his young friend, one among many, though with much more in his head than straw, a large part of it fear of discovery.

Doubting that he himself was an object for their attention, Monroe appeared to take no notice of the approaching security guards or of the straw men he had just left behind. He strolled back across the open space at a leisurely pace and found a spot behind a pen of several goats, where he faced the scarecrows. From a distance, Danny, holding perfectly still, blended in well with the stuffed group, and Monroe approved his effort to remain motionless.

The guards came closer, still searching the face of every boy of Danny's size and age, stopping every so often to question someone. The old man could imagine what they were asking: *Have you seen a boy of this description?* Without positive results, they came closer.

Two goats, curious and hoping, he assumed, for a handout, wandered up to the bars of the pen next to where Monroe stood anxiously watching without appearing to do so. As the guards reached a point midway between him and Danny in their search, one turned his head to glance at the collection of scarecrows. Immediately Monroe used his cane to direct a swift poke at the flank of the nearest goat. It bleated in indignation at the unexpected assault and leaped away from the bars of the pen, bumping into another goat in the process, which elicited more audible protest.

The sudden scramble and noise from the goats drew the attention of both guards toward the pen, where an innocent-looking elderly man appeared wide-eyed in surprise at the sudden hullabaloo the animals were causing.

As one guard shrugged and made some comment to the other, Monroe used his peripheral vision to watch them move on toward the rear of the barn, working to keep a smile from his face. *This,* he thought to himself, *was actually almost fun, a game of sorts.* It had been a long time since he felt quite so young and diabolical.

"You have my sincere apology, Billy," he apologized under his breath to the animal that was now nosing its insulted flank. Turning away, he strolled around the pen to watch the two guards complete their search and exit through the barn's back door.

If they had stood where they had paused in the middle of the open space, directly opposite the group of scarecrows plus one, they would have been able to see, as he saw, *one* red-plaid-shirted straw man roll and sag his shoulders in an enormous sigh of relief.

• • •

You should have seen the tension leave Danny's face when he was sure they were gone," Monroe told the assemblage in Jessie's living room with a chuckle. "He made a very good addition to the scarecrow band, though—held completely still when necessary."

"Then I moved, and that little kid told his dad the scarecrows were alive," Danny added, remembering. "But his dad didn't believe him."

"That's correct. I had almost forgotten the incident," Monroe agreed. "The child's eyes, over his father's shoulder, were great saucers of amazement when you stood up and walked away from that gang of straw."

CHAPTER 11

Jessie's morning had been full of questions to be answered and items to sell in the Iditarod booth. She was surprised to find it was after noon when Joanne told her to take a break. Intending to make a visit to the animal exhibits, she left Tank with Joanne, knowing that, though well behaved, he would be unwelcome there.

Eating a quick lunch, she strolled across the central plaza toward the barn, enjoying the fact that the threatened rain had not put in an appearance and the afternoon was warm and sunny.

A crowd had gathered near the sand sculpture, where its creator was back at work shaping and smoothing his medium. The people stood in a large circle but were not watching the sculptor. Instead they were focused on a young juggler on a unicycle that raised him perhaps six feet in the air. Skillfully he balanced himself on the single wheel and kept three flaming torches spinning in the air while he provided a humorous verbal patter that kept his audience laughing.

Jessie paused to watch before going on toward the barn at the edge of the plaza. Just before she reached the building, her attention was caught by two alpacas in a pen beside a booth that was selling sweaters and other items knit from their fleece. The black alpaca had been recently sheared, except for its tail and the top of its head. The other had been left fluffy with white fleece so soft it seemed unreal when Jessie put a hand between the bars of the pen to touch it. The animal had a shaggy fringe of black on top of its head that hung down in front, almost obscuring its vision. But it was the huge eyes of the animals that attracted her. With no definition between pupil, iris, or sclera, they were so completely dark that it was difficult to tell where the alpacas were looking. Framed with incredibly long lashes, their eyes reminded Jessie of still pools of water that gleamed with reflections on the surface but kept the secrets of their depths. So calm and slow-moving they seemed almost sleepy, the two animals stood staring into the distance beyond those who stopped to admire them, but she had a feeling that their enigmatic liquid eyes missed very little of what went on around them.

Entering the barn, Jessie stopped to decide what to see first. A long line of children stood waiting to gain entrance to the petting zoo, where only a few were allowed in at any one time. Taking a right, she entered a separate section of the barn reserved for poultry, rabbits, and some exceptional achievements of the area's local vegetable gardeners, including a cabbage that had weighed in at 70 pounds. *Enough sauerkraut for the whole winter,* she thought with a smile. Next to it was a list of other vegetable giants from years past: a 347-pound pumpkin, a 29-pound zucchini, a 75-pound rutabaga. Rich earth and the extended daylight of northern summer months were of great assistance to folks who babied their vegetables into such mammoth sizes.

Beyond the vegetables, the majority of the large room was taken up with poultry and rabbits. Jessie stopped to admire a pair of domestic geese and a turkey so enormous it almost filled its cage. Though most turkeys raised for the market seemed to be white, this one could have posed for a traditional Thanksgiving picture. Its naked head and wattle were mottled red and blue and a snood hung over its bill. The rest of the bird was covered with dark feathers, and as Jessie watched, it spread its tail and strutted proudly within its narrow confinement.

Continuing toward the back of the room, she passed by dozens of cages of rabbits of varied colors and types, after which a door led her back into the main part of the barn. There the cows, sheep, goats, pigs, llamas, more alpacas, and other domestic animals were confined in successive pens.

She was about to leave and head back to her job at the booth when she noticed a group of people that with much laughter and enthusiasm were working on something in a clear space along one side of the barn. Walking over to take a look, she found they were taking part in a scarecrow-building contest: creating humorous figures out of straw and items of used clothing—jeans, plaid shirts, floppy hats—that looked as if they had been rescued from the nearest thrift store. Several of the humorous figures had already been completed and propped against the wall, and Jessie couldn't help being amused at the empty, exaggerated grins painted with markers on some of the faces.

Until she glanced at her watch, she briefly considered making a scarecrow of her own, but noticing the time, she hurried back out of the barn. Taking the most direct route to the Iditarod booth, she found Joanne standing outside next to the truck that had been donated as the raffle prize, smiling at a man to whom she had just sold a ticket.

"Good luck," she told him as he walked away, then turned to Jessie. "Hey, how was the farm exhibit? I haven't been over there yet."

"Pretty good," Jessie told her, "but it seemed a little low on animals this year. There're some great scarecrows, though. You should take a look."

Inside the booth, Jessie stepped behind the counter to see if Tank needed more water in the pan she had left for him. The pan was there—half full. But her lead dog was not.

"Where's Tank?" she asked, turning to search the rest of the booth, figuring he had moved, or been moved, to some other corner.

"Isn't he right there? He was just a few minutes ago," Joanne said, frowning.

"Well, he's not now, or anywhere else in here."

They stood staring at each other, startled and confused, then turned quickly to look again, sure they must have missed the husky in the shadows among the displays of sweatshirts and jackets or behind the case of pins, mugs, and belt buckles. The water pan was still the only evidence that Tank had been there at all. He and his leash were missing.

Jessie could feel her heart pounding, and a lump of apprehension in her throat made it hard to swallow. Sled dogs were worth hundreds, sometimes thousands of dollars, especially leaders, and particularly those that had proved themselves in famous races like the Iditarod or Yukon Quest, both of which Tank had run and for which he had been prominently featured in the media. Many people in Alaska were well aware of this, and a few had been unscrupulous about making use of that knowledge in the past. Dogs had been stolen before. Some turned up eventually, but others had vanished forever. Taken out of state, to the northern Midwest, for instance, where many people ran dog teams, they could bring a lot of money to a thief if sold to some unprincipled person who would know enough never to bring them back to Alaskan races.

But it wasn't a simple case of Tank's value that pushed Jessie close to tears of dread, though that might be a reason for someone to steal him. Jessie had raised her favorite lead dog from a puppy, and the affectionate pair had spent years together. Running with a sled or not, they were almost always together, and they were well matched in temperament. Having him suddenly absent left her feeling empty and separate in a distinctly unfamiliar way, as abandoned as if Tank had purposely gone somewhere without her.

She was frightened and worried that whoever had taken him—and she was quickly becoming sure that someone had—would not treat him well. Not everyone likes dogs, and in her estimation a dog's welfare would not be a priority of anyone who would steal one for personal gain. They would be interested only in how much he was worth. She loved this dog. It made her sick not to know who had taken him, or where.

All this went through Jessie's mind as she hurried to the front of the booth and out onto the walkway to look carefully in both directions. Nothing.

"Was there anyone here while I was gone who seemed particularly interested in Tank?" she demanded of Joanne, returning to the booth. "Anyone at all?"

"Not that I noticed. There were only a few people who stopped. At least half of those didn't even go inside, just bought raffle tickets. I know I'd have seen anyone who came out with a dog. Maybe Tank just wandered off to look for you."

But Jessie had told Tank to stay, and she knew he would never have *wandered off* on his own. One of her most dependable dogs, he always stayed where she left him. However long it was, he would not have moved unless someone took him away.

But she knew that he, like all her dogs, was used to having other people around and to taking a certain amount of guidance from them. More than one handler periodically helped out at Jessie's kennel, which often included moving dogs to and from training teams and their places in the yard. Junior mushers sometimes came to gain experience by working with Jessie, learning how to care for their own dogs by helping out with hers.

"There was a boy here this morning—nine or ten years old, I think. He had brown hair and eyes, and his name was Danny. Do you remember?"

"Yeah, he was asking you questions about the Iditarod while he petted Tank."

"Right. He didn't come back, did he?"

Jessie hated to ask. Remembering how polite and considerate Danny had been about asking permission before he touched Tank, she couldn't imagine him taking the dog. Still, he had told her how much he wanted a dog of his own. *I'd like one just like him.* Was it possible? She thought it improbable, but felt she had to ask nonetheless.

"I didn't see him again," Joanne responded thoughtfully. "Let's ask around. Maybe someone here close to us saw something."

In a few minutes the two women had checked with all the surrounding vendors who might have noticed someone with a dog on a leash, but to no avail. Jessie was now beginning to grow a little frantic.

"We need help," she told Joanne. "I'm going to security."

The main office of security for the fair stood in the center of the grounds. Dozens of employees worked out of it round the clock to make sure exhibits, rides, vendors, and shows ran smoothly and the thousands of people who visited them were protected and as safe as possible. They worked hard to supervise the gates and pubs, settle disputes, pick up shoplifters, discourage rowdies and drunks, find lost children, and generally manage just about any problem that arose. Any serious crime or situation they could not or should not handle was referred to the Palmer Police Department. A second cabin next door was headquarters for teams of EMTs and paramedics, who coordinated with security to provide assistance in case of emergency, accident, or illness.

Jessie was glad to have security spring into action within minutes after she reported Tank's disappearance and the circumstances surrounding it. The director, Dave Lomax, a tall, competent man of about forty, seemed to take her report seriously and immediately sent a guard to each of the gates to see if anyone at the exits had noticed someone leave the grounds with a dog. If not, they were to report back on the radio each carried, then remain on watch.

Almost immediately one of them reported that one of the ticket sellers had earlier seen a man with a dog pass. But even as the report was being made, the person she had seen turned out to be a blind man with a German shepherd guide dog, not an Alaskan husky.

"Whoever took him might still be here on the grounds somewhere. You don't know exactly when the dog disappeared, do you?" Lomax asked Jessie as, at his suggestion, they began a search of the fair on foot.

"He was last seen by Joanne Potts at the Iditarod booth less than an hour ago," she told him. "I came back to the booth about ten minutes later, so he's been gone well over half an hour."

He frowned in thought as they walked on after fruitlessly questioning the guard who was checking identification at The Sluice Box and several surrounding vendors.

"Plenty of time to leave the grounds, if he went straight

from the booth to the gate. Whoever took Tank would have to be stupid to stay around, knowing a prizewinning sled dog would be missed in a hurry. And from what you've told me, someone *must* have taken him. You're sure he wouldn't have wandered away, and I think you're right. A pet? Maybe. Not a well-trained lead dog."

Ten minutes later they were passing the barn on their way to the equestrian center when Lomax's radio crackled to life with another reported dog sighting. They doubled back to a booth near the central plaza and spoke to a food vendor, who had noticed a husky on a leash with a man in jeans, a blue shirt, floppy hat, and dark glasses. "He went between the booths over there," he told them, pointing south. "I was busy with a customer, so I didn't pay much attention."

"Would you recognize this man if you saw him again?" Lomax asked.

"Probably not. Half the crowd is in jeans—lots of blue shirts. The hat and glasses hid most of his face."

The heart-stopping part of his description of the canine with this man, however, was that it had been wearing an orange bandana. Jessie's heart sank. If Tank had been taken off the grounds already, how would she ever find him? Her anxiety increased, making her feel a little sick to her stomach.

"What are we going to do?" she asked, feeling frustrated and stymied. "I think maybe it's time to involve the police in this."

"Don't you think we should keep on looking for a while longer?" Lomax asked when they had gone between the booths the vendor had indicated but found nothing but an access road next to the employee parking lot. They turned back toward the security office, and Jessie wondered a little at his hesitation about involving official law enforcement but put it down to a disinclination to entertain the idea that he couldn't solve her problem. It wasn't the first time she had become aware of territorial tension between the security and the police.

"By now, my guess is that we're trying to close the barn door after the horse—well, you know," Jessie told him. "The police can put out a bulletin so their patrols can be looking on the roads for someone with a husky in their vehicle."

Lomax nodded a bit reluctantly without answering, and they headed for the security office.

Approaching it, they passed a trailer that housed the Alaska State Troopers fair exhibit, and Jessie was surprised to see her friend trooper Phil Becker there. In full dress uniform, which required the absence of his favorite western hat, he was answering questions from the people who flowed past the exhibit. It was a part of community relations that she knew he enjoyed less than his usual job as a homicide detective, but he was very good with people and was often called upon to help out. Here was someone she knew would help and who also knew her dog. Without hesitation she made a quick right turn away from Dave Lomax and hurried to where Becker was standing next to a parked patrol car on which the roof lights flashed to attract the attention of fair goers.

"Phil," she told him simply, "someone's stolen Tank."

• • •

So that's when you got involved, Phil. Commander Swift had pulled rank and made you get spiffed up to make nice with the folks."

"Yeah. But it didn't last long after Jessie came and told me Tank was missing. I reassigned myself PDQ and got one of the new boys to take over the duty."

"But you didn't find Tank."

"Not because we didn't look. We had an army of people looking for him—all the security staff on the grounds, several PPD and AST officers on site. Anyone on patrol outside the fair got the word by radio. All we found at that time was a blue shirt that had been wadded up and tossed on the ground beside a station wagon in the employees parking lot. We tracked down the guy who owned the wagon, but he'd driven in just a little while before without seeing anything and obliterated the tire tracks of whoever had left the space empty. I thought then, and was proved right later, that the guy who took Tank went directly to his vehicle, drove off the grounds, and was gone. No one checks vehicles leaving *the grounds, especially those with employee passes on their windshields. They just wave them through to keep traffic moving. Hundreds of workers come and go from that lot all day long. So we had no way of knowing what kind of vehicle we were looking for or what direction he might have taken."*

"What did you do, Jessie?"

She shrugged and shook her head, as if feeling the frustration and dread that had accompanied her everywhere that horrible afternoon.

"I kept walking around, asking anyone I saw and hoping to get a clue from someone. I stayed all afternoon, until I couldn't

think of anywhere I hadn't looked several times over. At about seven I finally went home, and that was even worse—awful. Except for a night or two when Tank stayed over at the vet for some reason, I've hardly ever been at home without him. I worried about him all the way out Knik Road.

"Then, when I pulled into my driveway, Maxie McNabb's motor home was parked by the house. I was so glad to see her I almost cried."

CHAPTER 12

"It was so good to have someone there," Jessie went on. "The idea of being in my empty house and yard didn't seen right at all, but there was really no use in staying at the fair. I decided to go home and try to figure out something else to do. If he'd been taken off the grounds, there had to be somewhere else to look for Tank."

When Jessie's pickup pulled into the driveway, Maxie McNabb was rocking comfortably in a chair on the porch of her friend's new log house. Her reddish-brown toy dachshund, Stretch, had been snoozing at her feet, but at the sound of the vehicle he scrambled to the top of the steps and began to bark at whoever was coming in his direction. Several of the few sled dogs left in Jessie's yard also turned their attention to the arrival of their mistress. Only one met the stranger's frenetic challenge with a halfhearted woof or two in lower tones. The rest raised their heads, recognized the truck, and cast disdainful glances at this small foreign bundle of energy's demented behavior.

Maxie stood up and came down the steps and toward the truck with a welcoming smile and wave.

"Hush up, you silly galah," she told the dachshund. "It's Jessie come home finally, and nothing you need to make such a fuss about."

Stretch, quiet for the moment, trotted along at her side, his short legs a blur of motion.

Jessie shut off the engine of the pickup and leaned for a moment on the steering wheel as a rush of thankfulness swept over her for the answer to a prayer that she hadn't realized she'd made until she saw her friend.

The sixty-two-year-old woman had become special to Jessie on a trip up the Alaska Highway earlier that year. They had driven separate motor homes up the long road north but camped together a number of times and enjoyed each other's company. Inadvertently they had been drawn into a lengthy and dangerous chase involving a teenage boy from Montana who had become the target of a murderer who considered him a threat. Through it all they had found they had much to share, including their independence and positive outlooks, and knew they would continue to keep in touch.

Upon reaching Alaska, Maxie had gone on to Homer, on the Kenai Peninsula, where home meant a house on solid ground in a place where the Kenai Mountains rose in a vision of glaciers and peaks south of the wide waters of

Kachemak Bay. This inherited structure had been built by her father and was where she had been born and raised. There she had outlived two husbands: Joe Flanagan, her high school sweetheart, who had drowned in the storm that sank his commercial fishing boat; and Daniel McNabb, Australian expatriate, from whom Maxie had picked up the bits of Aussie *slanguage* that frequently enlivened her speech.

Three years earlier, reaching the end of her fifties, she had decided to see some of the rest of the world, bought a thirty-two-foot Jayco motor home she called her "gypsy wagon," and taken off to wherever appealed to her wanderlust and could be reached by road. For almost two years she had spent little time in Alaska, so after a winter in the high desert of New Mexico, she had been glad to have several months to renew old friendships and see to her neglected garden.

She had assured Jessie she would stop to visit on her way back down the highway to the Lower Forty-eight, and here she was, keeping that promise.

As Jessie climbed out of the truck, she was pleased to see that Maxie looked rested and fit from her summer of relaxation and gardening. She wore her preferred traveling costume of denim skirt with large patch pockets and an oversized blue shirt with sleeves rolled to the elbow. The brown moccasins on her bare feet almost matched the color of her dog, and her own hair, a salt-and-pepper blend, was pulled back into its usual heavy braid, more dark brown than gray. Her eyes sparkled with good humor and pleasure in anticipation of Jessie's company.

"Hello," she called in the low and vibrant voice that always reminded Jessie of a cello's rich tones. "It's about time you showed up. I was about to break out the Jameson's without you."

Recognizing a previous acquaintance, Stretch, wriggling all over, tail wagging furiously, dashed ahead to reach Jessie first. Rewarding him with a quick pat, she then enfolded Maxie in a huge hug.

"Oh," she said as the face of her friend swam through her tears, "you have no *idea* how glad I am to see you."

Taking a step backward, Maxie held the younger woman at arm's length to make an assessment of the distress that showed clearly on her face, and her welcoming smile turned quickly to an expression of concern.

"My dear. Whatever is wrong?"

As Jessie swallowed hard and swiped at her cheeks with the backs of her hands, Maxie took her firmly by the elbow and marched her toward the steps of the house. "Never mind for now. There's no need to stand yabbering in the yard when we can settle comfortably with a soothing shot of plonk. Once we're in, you will tell me all about it. Yes?"

Jessie nodded, relieved to have someone else take charge for a change, especially Maxie, whose practical judgment she had learned to trust, for good reason.

"Good. Come along then."

Up the steps they went. Jessie unlocked the door and they went inside, bringing Stretch along. While Jessie started a small fire in her cast-iron stove, he pattered around in a detailed exploration of this new space. Maxie located glasses in the kitchen and poured them both a generous portion of the Jameson's she had retrieved from her motor home.

"Now," she said, handing Jessie a glass and seating herself on one end of the huge sofa near the stove, yanking a green and blue pillow behind her for better support, "I'm guessing this has something to do with Tank, as he isn't in the yard and didn't come home with you."

"Yes," Jessie agreed. "He's gone, Maxie. Someone took him from the Iditarod booth at the fair, and he's disappeared completely. We have no idea who or why—or where he might have gone, for that matter. It all seems to be a dead end."

Maxie listened intently as Jessie described the events of her terrible afternoon and its lack of results, her words pouring out in a flood of anxiety and frustration that told the older woman the pain of the situation, though knowing how close Jessie was to her lead dog, she was already taking it very seriously. After asking the obvious questions about the search and who was involved, she heard about the shirt found in the employees' parking lot and Becker's speculations concerning it.

"No wonder you're upset," Maxie said when Jessie finished talking. She sat silently for a minute, frowning in thought. "If whoever it was drove away from the fairground, it can't have been the boy you mentioned, who's too young to drive. Are there any other suspects at all?"

"Not really, and I've been racking my brain all afternoon. People in the racing world are more familiar with the worth of a good lead dog, but offhand I can think of very few mushers I could suspect of stealing one."

"Hm-m." Maxie weighed the answer. "How about someone peripherally connected—someone who's dropped out of racing, or would like to get into it; a handler, a race volunteer? A lot of volunteers come from out of state for the Iditarod—even from out of the country."

Jessie sighed in frustration. "Not at this time of year. Besides, there would be hundreds on that list. I'm more inclined to think it's someone local."

"Have you considered that it might not be connected to mushing at all?"

"Yes—the ROW, as a pilot friend calls it—the rest of the world. And that leaves even more possibilities."

"But few would have a reason to snatch a dog. Maybe we should be thinking of reasons, not suspects."

They sat without speaking for a moment or two, both thinking hard. Then Maxie sat up and started to say something, hesitated, and fell silent, frowning.

"What?" Jessie asked, alert and wary. "What are you thinking? Say it."

"You're absolutely sure it couldn't be the boy?"

"Danny? I really don't think so. He just didn't strike me as that kind of kid, but he did say he had a friend."

"A friend you didn't see, right? Would Tank have gone off with the boy?"

Jessie considered, not liking to admit that it was possible. "Yes. I let Danny pet and feed him, which usually means—to almost any of my dogs—that I trust that person, so they would, too. He probably would have gone with Danny."

"Perhaps you should—"

What Maxie had been about to say was interrupted by the phone ringing behind them on a table against the wall. She waited while Jessie hurried to answer it, obviously hoping it was some word about her lead dog.

"Arnold Kennels, Jessie speaking."

For long seconds there was the empty sound of an open line, then a gruff voice that she didn't recognize growled alarming words into her ear.

"You want your dog back? Then listen up."

"Who is this?" Jessie demanded.

"Negative. I said *listen!* You got that?"

She took a deep breath and gave Maxie, who had stood up at the bewilderment in her friend's voice, a startled and frightened look. "Yes, I've got it. What—?"

"Just shut it," he snarled in her ear. "You want your dog, then find that kid and get a red camera bag from him. I get the bag—you get your dog. Now—"

"What bag?" Jessie asked. "I don't know anything about a red bag. What boy?"

"Then you'd better find out, hadn't you? You know which kid. He was there this morning, came out of the booth with a plastic sack in one hand. That kid stole the bag, so he'll know where it is, and you're gonna get it back for me. If you don't, that's it for the mutt."

"But—"

"No funny business. No cops. I'll be watching and listening, and I'll call you tomorrow night. Got it?"

"They're already looking for—"

But he had hung up abruptly and was gone.

For a silent moment, Jessie stared at the receiver in her hand, then dropped it in its cradle and came back to collapse onto the sofa, pale-faced and speechless.

"What?" Maxie questioned. "Who *was* that?"

Jessie ran her fingers through the blond waves of her hair, leaving it in disarray, and held her head between both hands in confusion and concern.

"I don't know *who* it was, but whoever it is, he's got my dog. It has something to do with Danny and a red camera bag."

Maxie listened as she poured out the gist of the phone conversation and her reactions to it, liberally mixed with four-letter words of frustration and anger. When she fell silent and sat pounding one knee with her fist, the older woman took a long look at her, then stood up, ready for action.

"All right. Now you call your trooper friend—Becker, is that it?"

"No!" Jessie responded sharply. "He said, 'No cops.' He also said he'd not only be watching, but listening. I think that might mean I'd better not use the phone, don't you?"

"Then use this." Reaching into one ample pocket, Maxie took out her cell phone and handed it over. "But he's not got your phone tapped, Jessie. That would be far too much trouble for a thing like this—planning ahead of time. If you were called at the last moment to work at the fair, he couldn't have known you'd be there—or that you'd have Tank with you. To me it seems more like someone taking advantage of a convenient opportunity."

"I hope you're right." Jessie, reluctant still, took the cell phone and, with Maxie nodding encouragement, punched in the number of the state troopers' office in Palmer.

CHAPTER 13

It was a good thing you came to the phone," Jessie told Phil Becker with a smile. "I had very mixed feelings about telling you anything after the warning in that call. If you hadn't been right there, I might have changed my mind."

"I'd gone back to my office when I saw there wasn't much more to be done at the fair," he explained. "It was obvious that Tank had been taken off the grounds. We had put out an APB and interviewed every fair worker we could think of who might have seen anyone leaving with a sled dog." He turned to Danny's parents, who sat across the room. "That was when I met Mr. and Mrs. Tabor, who had come in to report that their son hadn't been home since the previous afternoon."

Giving Frank Monroe a half-amused, half-rueful look, he included him as well. "It got even more complicated when your nephew showed up with the administrator of the senior center and reported you missing, too."

Monroe shrugged and smiled, fingering the stem of the pipe he had allowed to burn out as he listened to Jessie. "I guess it was too much to hope that I might be left alone," he sighed in obvious regret. "I'm actually amazed it took them so long to call out the militia. It was very convenient for them all to give credence to the theory that I haven't so much as a marble left rattling around in the cranium."

"Well, I got the impression that the administrator hadn't wanted to admit they had no idea where you were until it was clear they were coming up empty. She didn't call your nephew until you'd been gone almost twenty-four hours."

"Typical. They should be running a kindergarten" was Monroe's unrepentant comment.

There were sympathetic nods from the gathering, all remembering that they would be old someday. Becker turned back to Jessie.

"I wish you'd been able to record that call," he told her, "or that I'd had the time to come out there. After that things got really *complicated."*

"Wait—wait." The other trooper raised a restraining hand. "Before that, the word went out at the fair on both missing persons. And that was the night you first talked to me about Tank's disappearance, right?"

"Right. We printed up a couple of flyers with pictures of both Mr. Monroe and Danny Tabor and a description of Danny's bicycle and had security plaster them all over the grounds that night. We didn't get results until the next morning, though, when several people reported seeing them as a pair."

"We didn't see *those flyers until the next morning," Monroe interjected in apologetic defense. "If I'd known how seriously the Tabors were taking Danny's absence, I would have made him either go home or to the security office."*

"What did *you do?"*

"That night?"

"Yes."

"By the time the mug shots were distributed and stuck up everywhere, we had already proceeded to secret ourselves beneath the tables for a tranquil night of unsuspecting slumber."

"But we were running low on snacks," Danny stated, making sure everyone knew what was important to him.

"It was so busy that I had someone bring my dinner to the office that night," Becker recalled. "I was seriously concerned with that threatening phone call. But on top of it, I had a murder victim and two missing persons to deal with: a child and—pardon me, Frank—a senior citizen who was represented to me as dangerously incompetent. They seemed to take precedence at the time."

"Ha!" Monroe exclaimed in disgust. "Do I seem incompetent or dangerous?"

"Not at all. But at the time I had nothing to go on except what they told me. If anything had happened to bear out their assessment—if you'd been sick or injured somewhere—and we weren't out looking for you, it could have come back to bite me big-time. So we posted the flyers on you both and started an area-wide search. Remember that at the time we didn't know for sure that either one of you was at the fair. We thought Danny probably was, because that's where his parents said he had wanted to

go. But you could have been anywhere. Patrol units were looking for a dog, a senior gentleman"—a nod to Monroe—"and a ten-year-old on a bicycle.

"Until later we had no real clue that any of this was related. We had a dead man, and we had a dog and two people reported missing, but nothing to tie them together. If I'd heard the part of your story, Jessie, that included Danny coming to the Iditarod booth earlier in the day, I might have connected it because of the name. But I didn't come out to your place that evening, so that part got lost in the shuffle. I had enough information from you about the threatening phone call to start looking into it, but I simply had too much on my plate otherwise. It's like that sometimes. You wind up doing a balancing act, keeping things together by taking care of necessities for each case but not getting to anything in depth. Besides, I wasn't worried about you. I knew you had someone there with you—your friend, right?"

He's really busy," Jessie told Maxie as she came back to the sofa and sat down next to the older woman. "But at least he knows." She grimaced and rubbed at her injured knee, which was aching from all the walking she had done at the fairground in search of information about her lost dog. She started to get up. "I've got to get some ice on this knee."

"Sit still," Maxie told her. "I'll get it."

She got up and headed for the kitchen, her dachshund trotting along beside her.

"Put a bowl of water down for Stretch," Jessie suggested.

"Good idea."

At Jessie's direction, Maxie found what she needed to put

an ice pack together and water her dog. She then refilled their glasses and handed Jessie the painkiller for her internal and external hurts.

"I hope telling Becker doesn't get Tank killed," Jessie fretted. "But he already knew that Tank was missing. The guy on the phone hung up before I could tell him so. There's another thing that worries me. There was a *Daily News* reporter there this afternoon, and we told him everything, hoping that somebody who reads the paper would know or see something that would help. It's going to be in tomorrow morning's edition. When this guy sees it, he may think I didn't take what he told me seriously."

"You have to ignore it. I don't think this is something you can do alone. Anyway, law enforcement has more resources, *and* they know how to handle this kind of situation.

"Damn! I wish I could stay and help you, but I've got to take off in the morning."

Jessie had scooted back and lifted her leg onto the sofa to apply the ice pack. Now she looked up sharply, disappointment evident on her face. "Oh, no. Even if all this wasn't going on, I thought you'd be able to stay for at least a couple of days."

"Me, too. But an old friend of mine is dying in Colorado. She called me two days ago to ask if I would be executor of her estate. It's an odd situation. There are things she said she couldn't tell anyone else but refused to tell me on the phone. So I'm going to be pushing it to get there as fast as possible and *must* leave tomorrow. I'm sorry, Jessie. She and I went to college together, and I promised."

Knowing Maxie, Jessie realized that she made few promises and never lightly, nor did she break them once made. It was a trait she admired.

"Don't worry about it," she told her. "I'll be fine. And so will Tank, I hope. With Becker and company on the case, we'll get this guy. What could you do anyway but be moral support?"

Maxie gave her a stern and motherly look. "Don't underestimate moral support," she replied.

"Yes, ma'am."

They both smiled for the first time since Jessie's arrival.

"I've got the tail half of a fresh salmon in the Jayco," Maxie told her. "Thought we could bake it up with some lemon, onion, and cream cheese. What do you think? I'll cook."

"You're on." Jessie realized she hadn't eaten since lunch and was seriously hungry. It seemed days had passed in the time between.

While the salmon baked, Maxie made a salad, and they talked of things unrelated to trouble or to Tank's disappearance. Maxie's summer in Homer and the condition of her garden: "Not half bad. The beds were grotty but cleaned out fine with help from a neighbor boy. Wish I'd had a bit longer to harvest the veggies, but I left them for his mother." The building of Jessie's new log house: "It went up like a set of Lincoln Logs, and after I hurt my knee, almost everybody I know came to help with the finish work. I'm lucky to have so many friends."

"You know," Maxie said when they had finished with dinner and were seated once again on the sofa, Jessie with another ice pack on her knee, "some time this winter, since you won't be racing, you should fly down and spend some time with me."

"Where will you be?"

"Not sure yet. Part of it depends on Sarah and how it goes in Grand Junction. But I'll let you know. In fact, I'll call you as I go down the road."

"If I'm not here, leave a message?"

"Absolutely. And I'll let you know where I decide to land."

She went to Jessie's desk and found a scrap of paper on which to write her cell phone number, which she pinned to the bulletin board above the phone. "Don't forget that between Canadian towns it's impossible to reach me on the cell. I'll call in the evening. I want to know what's going on and when you get Tank back."

"Your lips to God's ear," Jessie said bravely. "Oh, Maxie, I just wish I knew where he is. I'd figure out how to just go get him and to hell with the idiot that took him."

"Then it's probably good that you don't know." The older woman sat back down and gave Jessie another serious glance. "I guess you could hide one dog almost anywhere," she said, taking a sip of after-dinner coffee. "But if someone who didn't usually have a dog showed up next door to me—especially someone with an Alaskan husky—and I'd seen in the paper that one had been stolen, I'd be calling the police. Wouldn't you?"

"This guy might not live right next door to someone else."

"True. He may also hide Tank in some isolated place for that very reason."

"Or . . ." Jessie's eyes narrowed as an interesting thought crossed her mind.

"What?"

"Well—if I were trying to hide a dog, what better place than with other dogs—other sled dogs?" She sat up, excited with her sudden flash of inspiration. "I'd put him in—"

"—a kennel," Maxie finished. "That's a crash hot idea. But I don't think you should—"

"—go look?" Jessie interrupted. "Probably not, but what could it hurt to drive by a few local kennels before I go back to the fair, as long as I stay in the truck and don't tangle with whoever took him? If they want money for him, then whoever has him must be somewhere in the area and not too far away. Wouldn't they try to get him out of sight in a hurry after they took him—away from where he might be recognized? A local dog yard makes sense."

Maxie shook her head, frowning. "I know you, remember? And I know that you're not programmed to sit on your hands and hope this thing solves itself. You're as game as Ned Kelly, and I admire that. But you can't go off half cocked in just any old direction and hope to be successful."

"I won't," Jessie promised. "It's a long shot anyway, but I might just find him, you know? And I will be very careful."

So that's what got you out cruising the valley, looking at every kennel within driving distance—and into deep trouble," Becker *said. “How many times have I told you not to go off on your own, Jessie?”*

“Lots.” She grinned impishly. “But it was *obviously a reasonable idea. I waved Maxie off the next morning early, fed my mutts, then decided I'd just drive around and take a look at some dog yards—and in the process get the word out to mushers I know that Tank was missing.”*

“Meanwhile,” Becker continued, “I was at the fairground meeting with Danny and Frank, who had finally decided to give themselves up. By the time I got to your place, you were nowhere to be found.”

“I left a note for Billy.”

“Thanks for small favors. It at least told me when you had expected to be back.”

CHAPTER 14

"That was the morning my bicycle was gone," Danny said suddenly, sitting up so abruptly that he woke Tank, who sat up as well to see what was going on. "I thought somebody stole it."

"They found your bicycle earlier that morning," his father told him, "when they came to get straw and knocked over the pile of bales. They stumbled over the bike when they were piling them up again. When they brought it to the security office the director called us."

"That really frightened us, Danny," Mrs. Tabor spoke up. "Knowing how much you love that bicycle, we thought something must have happened to make you leave it. When nobody could find you, we didn't know what to think."

"Sorry," Danny muttered, once again ducking his head.

"So after you saw the flyers we'd posted, you went to the security office?" Becker asked, turning to Frank Monroe.

"Very soon after that. With one of their own security people involved, I was uncertain about confiding to them what I had discovered about his connection to the dead man. But before I was forced to relate much of what I knew, you showed up and took possession of the bag, camera, pictures, film—and, of course, us runaways."

"Lucky I did, considering what it eventually led to," Becker said, scowling at the ale bottle he had just emptied and held clutched in one hand. "I wouldn't have been able to take a look at those pictures, or figure out what they meant, if you'd returned the bag to its owner. It was also seeing how anxious he was to get it back that made me take another look at the contents. So I got there just in time. But I didn't really finish talking to Danny until later."

Frank Monroe nodded agreement. "I had already taken a look at the photos in the bag and thought them rather odd—even boring—but I hadn't seen the undeveloped ones. It didn't seem important enough to mention, considering the commotion everyone was making over us and the fuss the owner of that bag was making. I had a feeling there was something out of kilter about the death of his friend, but it was just a hunch, based more on his attitude than anything else, though I had seen the two of them together. But you didn't know that."

"Danny had seen them together, too, but I didn't know it then. I realized later that that's what made him dangerous. You were the only people who had seen the two of them together and could connect the guy with Belmont—especially Danny's observing the fight."

"Yes, but he knew he was in trouble with his parents and was being pretty quiet. He didn't mention that the two men were en-

gaged in a pugilistic encounter, or what he'd heard them say—just that he'd snatched the bag by mistake and been chased. You didn't know, so it didn't really make sense until later, did it?"

"Nope. With part of our guys on duty at the fair we were shorthanded, and it was a pretty busy morning that didn't allow me to focus on any one thing. I was concerned with delegating things other people could do, so I could get back to the murder at the fairground as soon as information came in from the crime lab. If I'd had more time, I would have asked more questions. We were in the middle of figuring out what to do with the two of you when Joanne called to tell me that Jessie should have been at the Iditarod booth over an hour before and still hadn't come in. She'd tried to call and was worried when all she got was Jessie's answering machine. So as soon as possible—after Danny's parents came to collect him—I offered you a ride back to the senior center, and you didn't seem to mind taking a quick ride out Knik Road to Jessie's first."

"Much to my appreciation, you didn't automatically accept the premise that I was senile," Monroe said, gesturing with his pipe. "I was in no particular haste to repair to my unlockable pigeonhole."

"Well," Becker assured him, "it was pretty easy to see that you were not even close to 'dangerously incompetent'! Seemed to me that you ought to have more control over your life than they were trying to allow you. It is yours, after all." He went on more sternly. "But Danny's under age, and that was another question. As a responsible adult, you should have either made sure he went home or reported him as a runaway."

"Oh, I suppose I should have," the old man agreed, a bit sheep-

ish in recalling his own behavior. "But we were both enjoying the adventure of it all, weren't we, Danny?"

"We sure were! At least most of the time. I sure didn't like that guy chasing me."

"But you won't do anything like that again, will you?" Danny's father demanded of his son.

"No, sir." But Danny's wide grin agreed with the old man's assessment of their escapades and answered the twinkle in his eye. "But can I visit Mr. Monroe sometimes?"

"I think that can be arranged," his mother said, smiling across at Monroe. "And maybe he could visit us, too."

"I'd enjoy that immensely," he agreed with a dignified bow of acceptance.

During the latter part of this discussion, John Timmons, the assistant coroner, had been listening silently from his place in the informal circle. Now he turned to Becker's trooper partner with a question.

"It was about that time that you showed up, wasn't it?"

The tall, lanky figure stirred in the rocking chair he occupied, uncrossed his jeans-clad legs, tugged at one end of his red-blond handlebar mustache, and leaned forward a bit as he glanced across the room at Jessie before answering Timmons.

"Not quite, but I was on my way," he said slowly. "It was later that afternoon that I arrived at the office in Palmer, fresh off a plane from Seattle."

Before leaving home that morning, Jessie had left a note for Billy Steward, the junior musher who helped care for the dogs in her kennel.

Billy,

I'll be back before ten, when I have to go help out at the fair. It's going to be a warm day, so please give the mutts more water. You could also start cleaning the old straw out of their boxes.

Thanks,
Jessie

The handler had evidently not yet arrived when Phil Becker found the note under the knocker on her front door. After reading it thoughtfully, he replaced it and left to accompany a resigned Frank Monroe back to the Palmer Senior Center for Assisted Living.

Back in his office at the Alaska state troopers' post, he sat down at his desk and spread out the items from the red bag that he had confiscated and brought with him. Though there seemed to be nothing but photographic equipment, the fact that its security guard owner, one Ron Wease, urgently wanted it back made Becker uneasy. So did Danny's limited tale of accidentally picking it up with his own while the two men were arguing behind The Sluice Box pub. Until he had time to go through it and consider the contents, he had been unwilling to release the bag. Now he intended to go through it all thoroughly.

There had been so much going on that until he reached Jessie's and found her gone, he really hadn't begun to consider the details of what she had reported the night before. "He said that some kid had stolen his camera bag and that if I want my dog back, I have to get it back for him," she had said. "Otherwise he'll kill Tank." It had, of course, occurred to Becker that the bag he held was probably the same bag Jessie's caller had demanded that she retrieve for him. Therefore it followed that Ron Wease could be her caller. What was so important about this bag and its contents? Did it have anything to do with the dead man found in the pond? In itself, an argument behind a pub was not an unusual occurrence, even if a few punches had been thrown. He wondered if either Danny Tabor or Frank Monroe could have identified the body that was now fifty miles away in the crime lab.

He was thumbing through the photographs from the bag and considering the rolls of exposed and undeveloped film when he heard the door of his office open. Looking up, he was pleased to find the long-legged figure of an old friend lounging casually against its frame, western hat in hand, self-satisfied grin on his face.

Dropping the pictures on the desk, Becker moved enthusiastically around it and reached to pump the hand of his former partner, who had taught him much of what he knew about homicide.

"*Jensen!* You old *rascal!* What the hell are you doing back in Alaska?"

"Oh, I just thought I'd take a chance that you might need a hand at catching bad guys up here."

The two stood grinning at each other until Becker waved Alex Jensen to a chair in front of the desk and regained his own behind it.

"What happened to the Idaho sheriff's job? I thought you

were committed to being Salmon's main man for a couple of years."

"Yeah, well—it wasn't working out quite the way I thought it would. They managed to corral somebody else, so I'm off the hook. I had a talk with Commander Swift on the phone, and he's willing to forgive my forays into the Lower Forty-eight and put me back to work."

"Terrific! When do you start?"

"Now, if you've got anything for me."

"Oh, yes! I definitely have something for you!" Becker slapped the surface of the desk with one hand in his relief at the unexpected assistance from a man he had worked with and trusted. "We've got a nasty homicide at the fairground. Someone used an ax to split the skull of a guy and leave him to float in the logrolling pond. The body was found yesterday morning, but he was probably killed the night before. Timmons is doing the post and will call as soon as he has anything."

Jensen had straightened in his chair, alert and focused on what Becker was telling him.

"What kind of an ax?"

"Big double-bladed sucker—the kind you use to make firewood out of logs. Sharp—belonged to one of the guys who does the lumberjack show twice a day, and they keep those things honed to a razor edge. Someone came up behind this guy and sank it halfway through his head. Driver's license in his wallet gave us ID. He's Curtis Belmont, a small-time hoodlum with a grand theft auto conviction."

"Nasty way to die, but quick."

"That's what Timmons said. Whoever used it clearly wasn't just trying to get the guy's attention."

"Prints on the ax?"

"Some from the guys in the show, who use and sharpen it every day, plus a couple unidentified that don't show up on any records. They printed all the show guys and are going back over what dabs there are, but it's unlikely they'll get anything else."

"Could one of the show guys be your perp?"

Becker shook his head and shrugged in frustration. "Maybe, but that's a stretch, isn't it?"

"Unless he hoped you'd think so."

"This one doesn't seem to have that kind of planning involved. I think it's more a case of opportunity—using a weapon that came to hand. Those axes are supposed to be locked up when they're not being used. But they say they could have missed one.

"We just don't know enough yet. Plus, I've got another couple of things on my plate from the fair. As I told you on the phone, Jessie's lead dog got swiped from the grounds yesterday."

Knowing that Jensen and Jessie Arnold had been a couple until six months earlier when Jensen had moved back to his hometown in Idaho to take a job as sheriff, Becker was now feeling his way with caution into unknown relationship territory that he felt was none of his business.

"Right," Jensen answered with an expression that gave away none of his feelings about Jessie. "Still missing?"

"Yes. Ah—listen, Alex. Does Jessie know you're back?

Have you seen her? Do you know why she wasn't home when I stopped by a while ago and didn't come to the fair this morning?"

"Did you expect her to be home?"

"Well—yeah. I mean—she didn't actually *say* she'd be there. She was supposed to be at the Iditarod booth but didn't show and didn't answer her phone, so I thought I'd better take a look. Found a note on her door that she'd be back by ten o'clock, but it was well after ten when I got there."

Jensen ran a hand through his blond hair and frowned. "Any idea where she went?"

"Not really. But I wouldn't put it past her to go looking for that dog of hers. You know how independent she is, and she was pretty upset when he turned up missing, especially after the phone call I told you about yesterday. Hell, it *was* just yesterday I told you, wasn't it? Yes, of course it was. How the hell did you get here so fast? And why didn't you tell me?"

Jensen stood up and walked to the window to look out at the mountains to the south that still had a patch or two of snow on their tall summits.

"Sorry I didn't let you know my plans, but it seemed like a nice surprise to just show up. I'd already talked to Swift and was coming anyway," he said over his shoulder. "So I just tossed a few more clothes in the duffel, drove to Missoula last night, and caught the last plane out for Seattle. From there it was only three hours this morning. After what you told me, I figured I might as well—"

The phone on Becker's desk interrupted with its summons.

"Becker. Oh, yes, sir."

Frowning and intent, he grabbed a pencil and began to scribble notes as he listened, gesturing Jensen back to his seat. "Yes, sir. Right away. He's here. I'll tell him."

He hung up the receiver and scowled at what he had written. "Commander Swift," he explained to Jensen. "Dammit. I think I was right about Jessie going looking for that dog on her own. Someone from Willow just reported a truck parked on the side of one of those roads near Nancy Lake. They've run the plate and it's hers, but no one there has seen her. He thinks we better check it out."

"What about the Belmont investigation?"

"We've done everything we can do at the scene. By the time we get back they may have more information for us from the lab."

Gathering the camera, photos, and film he had spread on his desk, Becker put them back in the red bag to take with them.

"I'll explain about this, but I'd like your take on it," he told Jensen. Handing over the bag, he grabbed a jacket as they went out the door.

CHAPTER 15

Danny's ride home with his parents had gone about as he expected it would. Both of them let him know exactly how angry and disappointed they were with his behavior.

Jill Tabor's anger, however, was mitigated with relief at having him back safely—the emotional residue of more than a day's imagination and worry over what might have happened to him. She kept reaching over the seat back to touch him, as if she wanted to be sure he was still there.

His father, on the other hand, let him know just how long he would be grounded for being so irresponsible—a month—and the chores he could expect to find added to his usual slate of duties. Mowing the lawn *twice* a week was high among them.

"That includes whacking the weeds around all the flower beds. And if I see so much as one single blade of grass over two inches high, you'll be out there on your knees with a pair of scissors, young man."

Danny slumped in silence in the backseat of the car and wondered if Mr. Monroe would be suffering the same kind of lecture. If so, he thought the old man would probably have a bigger word for it. He had terrific big words for everything.

"Alliance," he said softly to himself.

"What?" his father demanded.

"Nothing."

"Sit up straight," said his mother.

Frank Monroe was doing his best to ignore the harangue he was getting from his nephew and the administrator of the Palmer Senior Center for Assisted Living.

"You simply cannot take off without permission," his nephew had just stated in irritation, shaking his head and a finger in Monroe's direction. "It's not allowed."

"Permission? I need *permission* to leave this place?"

"Yes, Mr. Monroe," the administrator chimed in. "We must know where you are at all times. Read your contract. It states very plainly that we are responsible for transporting you and making sure you are safe and well."

"I don't recall the word *permission* appearing in anything I read or upon which I inscribed my signature."

"Well, perhaps the precise *word* is not stated, but the contract clearly implies that we have legal authorization to make decisions concerning your welfare, and that translates to—"

"It does not translate to keeping me in a cage," Monroe

told her flatly. "I am a person—not an animal to be counted, inspected at will, and hauled around like cargo."

"Don't be ridiculous," the nephew snapped. "I do not have time to be constantly searching for you all over town. Someone must be responsible for—"

"Then don't," Monroe told him.

"Don't?"

"Don't bother to waste your time searching for me. I'm perfectly capable of knowing where I am at any given time and taking care of myself. I don't need a keeper."

They suspended their confrontation of him long enough to give each other long-suffering looks. His nephew shrugged and raised his hands, palms up, as if to say, *I give up*.

The administrator decided to try one more time. "Mr. Monroe, we can't allow—"

"Look," he cut her off abruptly. "Evidently I have compounded the grave error in judgment I made by agreeing to reside here. I expected to be afforded privacy, some degree of dignity, and a modicum of the respect due an octogenarian with competent intelligence and a body that still functions adequately, thank you very much. Let us discontinue this debate. I will start with today's classified advertisements to find myself another, more suitable living arrangement."

"But you can't—"

The administrator broke in on his nephew, her voice now sharply impatient. "We *do* have a contract, Mr. Monroe. Besides, what if you have another heart attack? What if you forget to take your medication, trip over something, fall and injure yourself? You could lie alone for hours, and no one would know or come to help you. Don't you understand that?"

From her tone, he could almost have sworn she was hoping that any or all of what she had listed would happen to punish him for what she perceived as his stupidity.

"Well, then," he told her with a thin smile that did not reach his eyes, "I will have to lie there, won't I? But it will be a result of my decision and conduct, not yours—in my new residence, not yours. That should provide alleviation of your onerous burden of responsibility. You may anticipate hearing from my solicitor concerning our contractual agreement. And by the way, I have an extremely competent attorney, even if he is in his late sixties."

Once again settling his hat on his head at a jaunty angle, he rose.

"Now, I am going to retire to my *pigeonhole* to indulge in a much anticipated shower. Tell *Nurse Ratchet* to stay the hell out of my room. You may also inform her that my name is *Mr.* Monroe, or at the very least Frank—not *Frankie boy!* And for your edification, I had a minor stroke—a *transient ischemic attack*—not a *myocardial infarction.*"

Leaving them both staring after him, he strolled from the administrator's office and down the hall, swinging his cane and feeling better than he had in months—except, of course, for his time at the fair with Danny Tabor.

A most commendable alliance, he told himself, remembering.

It was much later that evening, after Danny Tabor had gone to bed without argument and his parents were settled in the living room to watch a movie on television, when a pickup cruised slowly along the street. Swinging around in the intersection at the end of the block, the driver took the pickup past again so he could get another look at the house.

"That kid," he said to his companion, Ron Wease, "is the only person who got a look at you and Curt behind The Sluice Box. We'll just tuck him away somewhere till we're through with this."

"Through with this, hell! We can't go through with this *now*."

"Why not? Curt's obviously not going to be a problem, thanks to you. And the kid won't be if we stash him—like the woman—maybe *with* the woman and that damned dog. What the hell were you thinking about with that *dog*, for shit sake?"

"I can think of a more permanent solution for the kid."

"But unnecessary—and unpleasant at the moment. It was stupid enough of you to leave Curt's body at the fairground, when there's thousands of miles of wilderness where it'd never have been found. This thing is going to go as planned, dammit. And nobody's going to suspect that *I* have anything to do with it. If you hadn't lost your temper with Curt, they wouldn't suspect you either. But you'll be long gone before they go looking for you."

"What about the photos? That cop has all the pictures I took."

"But you said that only one roll had been developed. They're just pictures of the fairground anyway."

"What if they develop the rest?"

"Why would they, and what if they do?"

Wease hesitated, thinking of one particular roll he had exposed that might be of interest to the police. "I dunno," he said with a scowl.

"So don't worry about it. You'll get your bag and camera stuff back, and that'll be it."

But Wease had other ideas. It was time, he thought, to opt out of this operation and disappear—now, not later. As they drove back through Palmer toward the fairground, he thought about it and made up his mind. The rest was only a matter of how to accomplish his vanishing act. Where he would go was something to figure out later. But he already knew it would be somewhere far away and out of reach—of this guy, as well as the police.

CHAPTER 16

Nancy Lake was a small community and recreation area approximately twenty-five miles northwest of Palmer along the Parks Highway between the towns of Houston and Willow. That particular stretch of the highway was an area popular with mushers, so it was scattered with their kennels and dog yards. There the noise of their dogs did not bother the neighbors, most of whom had dogs of their own. The residents lived either close to the highway or on the gravel roads that branched away from it, where immediate access to wilderness trails from the back of their properties made it especially attractive to dog team trainers. The area was a tangle of roads and the trails mushers had carved out of the forest to allow passage for sled dog teams.

Becker elected to take a direct bypass from Palmer to Wasilla and pick up the Parks Highway there rather than fight the endless traffic that was currently snarling all roads to the fairground. As he passed an intersection in the middle of Wasilla, he glanced toward Knik Road and swore.

"Damn. I should have gone out to Jessie's last night when she called instead of waiting till this morning. Maybe I could have talked her out of going out hunting on her own."

"Probably not." Jensen grinned. "She's inclined to run her own life, Phil. Wouldn't be Jessie if she . . ." He let the sentence die, keeping his assessment to himself, and turned his head to stare out the passenger window as they went by a gas station or two and the run-down North by NorthRest Motel on the outskirts of town.

Becker cast a sympathetic glance in his direction, speculating about the relationship between his two friends. But he wisely decided not to ask questions and for the moment let Jensen's thoughts remain his own. Still, he couldn't help wondering if—

"Tell me about this stuff." Jensen interrupted his friend's thoughts by turning to unzip the red bag that lay between them on the seat of the truck that Becker drove instead of a more revealing squad car.

"I was trying to mentally organize that stuff with other things when you showed up," Becker began. "Let me lay out what I know in the order it happened. Then maybe we can make sense of some of it. First, yesterday morning this guy Belmont was found dead in the pond in the small arena. Second, yesterday afternoon Jessie's dog was snatched at the fair. Third, we got a report from the Tabors that their son, Danny, had been missing since the day before. Fourth, another report came in about an old man, Frank Monroe, missing from the Palmer senior center for about the same length of time. We put up flyers with pictures and descriptions of both, with no results until today. Fifth, Jessie got that phone call at home last night from the guy that took her dog. Sixth, Danny and Frank Monroe turned themselves in at the fair security office this morning, and they *did* have the red bag with photography stuff in it. The boy said that Wease dropped it, and he picked it up accidentally. Ron Wease was there. He immediately interrupted what Danny was telling me and demanded it back, but I thought I'd better take a look to see why it was so important to him. He was adamant about wanting that bag right then. Didn't like it at all when I held on to it. He was still arguing with me about it when Danny's parents came in to get him."

"And it stands to reason that it's the same bag that was mentioned to Jessie in the phone call last night, so he must be the caller."

"Not established yet, but I have to agree that it's at least possible—even likely. But it's also possible that there's something about what's in it that would make it attractive to someone else. Proving it will be another thing. But Wease, of course, claimed he never called threats to anybody, and we can't prove he did."

Jensen sorted through the bag and took out the pictures that Becker had been examining earlier. Slowly he flipped through them and frowned, puzzled.

"Nothing much—just some snapshots of the crowd and buildings in the center plaza of the fair. Not even very interesting."

"Right. What I'd like to know is what's on those other rolls of film—the ones that have been exposed but not developed. Might tell us something else."

"We could send them to the lab and find out, but it'd be faster to drop them off at one of those places that develop film in an hour. But if there's nothing any more damaging than what we've already looked at, you'll have nothing. Unless you can prove that he called Jessie."

"And if he did, you can be sure it was from some pay phone."

"Might be from one at the fairground. They could run a check to see if any were made to Jessie's from those."

"Still wouldn't prove he made the call, if there was one. Must be a lot of calls made from those phones."

"Not so many as if half the world didn't carry their own cell phones. Now there's a thought. Does Wease have a cell phone?"

"True, to the first. I don't know, to the second. Let's get a look at what's on that film first."

So on the way back to town we dropped off the film," Jensen told the group. "First we spent a couple of hours hunting for Jessie and not finding her. Her truck had the keys still in it, as if she hadn't intended to leave it where it was for very long."

"I didn't," Jessie agreed. "I got out to take a look at a couple of kennels that were back in the trees where I couldn't see much from the road. But I was coming right back."

"That wasn't the only time you'd left the truck."

"No. When I knew the owner of a kennel, I'd drive in and hop

out to talk to them. I wanted word about Tank to reach as many mushers as possible—people who knew dogs and could be on the lookout for him."

Jensen nodded. "That particular road had half a dozen kennels along it. You could have gone to any one of them."

Jessie frowned and shook her head. "That's not right. There were only four kennels along the road where I left the truck, and I'd talked to two of them on the way in—Judy Clark and Mose Atkinson. I got out to take a look at one of the others, the third dog yard down that road, about a mile from Judy's place. I didn't see anyone around, but it was a terrible place. That's the last I remember."

"Lynn Ehlers got to Clark and Atkinson later and figured out that their road was the last place anyone could confirm seeing you that morning. There was still no one at the other kennel you went to. But Ehlers talked to the owner of the fourth kennel on that road—we interviewed him later. He said he had passed an unfamiliar truck headed out toward the highway as he was on his way in from a trip to town. Your truck was not found there, however. It was a mile east of that road, on another road on the other side of the highway."

They stared at each other, comprehension dawning.

"But I never got to the road you're describing," Jessie said, frowning.

"In that case it's no wonder everyone near where we found the truck denied seeing you," Becker broke in. "They hadn't. I'm sorry we gave them such a bad time. When we couldn't find you, we wound up driving your truck back to town and going over it top to bottom—with no results, I might add. Not a print on the wheel but yours."

"When we were through searching the truck for any idea where you were, I drove it out to your place while Phil went back to pick up the pictures," Jensen told her. "I thought you might show up or that there might be something inside your house to give me a clue where we should concentrate our search for you."

Alex Jensen drove Jessie's truck up the long driveway from Knik Road and parked it in front of her new log house. Shutting off the engine, he sat for a long minute appreciating the structure that had replaced the cabin that had burned several months earlier. The replacement was larger, more house than cabin, and its log walls and green metal roof were appealing, as were the steps and wide porch leading to the front door. But it felt odd, as if he had come back to a place with familiar anticipation only to find it subtly changed in ways that scrambled recognition.

It made him wonder if Jessie had experienced similar changes in the months he had been absent. If she had stepped out that front door to meet him, could he have expected a welcome?

Considering possible transformations in the woman and her environment, he removed the keys from the ignition, opened the door, and climbed out. Immediately, seeing a stranger instead of the person they expected to leave the pickup, several of the dogs began to bark. A human voice from the back of the dog yard startled him further.

"Shut up, you guys. Hey there, Alex."

Locating the source of the voice, he was pleased to find it was Billy Steward, Jessie's handler and kennel assistant, who was walking toward him from where he had been cleaning straw from dog boxes.

"Jessie's not here," Billy informed him, halting a few feet away, a rake in his hand. "She know you're home? I guess she must, you've got her truck."

Home. Jensen thought the word didn't accurately depict his presence, but let it pass.

"You see her today?" Jensen asked, knowing the answer but hoping anyway.

"Nope. She's at the fair, but she left me a note."

"Did you meet her friend who was here last night?"

"Didn't know anyone but Jessie *was* here. Why? Something wrong?"

Jensen, realizing that Billy didn't even know Jessie's lead dog was missing, related as much of the story as he knew, including where they had found her apparently abandoned truck.

"Ah, jeeze," the young man commented when he had heard everything Jensen had to tell. "She's gotta be really upset about Tank. What was she doing out the highway?"

"Looking for him would be my guess." He gazed over the empty spaces in the yard that usually held upward of forty dogs. "Where are the rest of her dogs, Billy?"

"Lynn Ehlers has them out the road in a kennel pretty close to where you found her truck. Jessie can't race this winter because she hurt her knee a couple of months ago and had to have surgery on it. Doctor told her not to even do training runs, so Lynn took her dogs for the winter."

"Ehlers? A musher from Minnesota?" Jensen asked,

thinking it might not hurt to check this Ehlers out, considering the location of the kennel Billy described.

"Yeah—friend of Jessie's. He helped out a lot when she got hurt." Billy looked at the ground and kicked at a pebble with one boot, clearly uncomfortable to be talking to Jensen about another male acquaintance of Jessie's. "You know him?"

"Met him during the Yukon Quest last February. He been around lately?"

"Not when I was here."

For a longish bit of silence, Jensen assessed the boy's discomfort, until Billy finally glanced up at him.

"Pete still keeper of the house key?"

"Yup."

Jensen stepped across to where Pete, a dog he knew well, lay dozing in the sunshine on top of his box.

"Hey, Pete. Good old boy." Taking time to give the old dog a pat or two and rub his ears, he reached into the box and retrieved the extra key to Jessie's front door from a hook hidden inside.

"I'm going in to see if there's anything that will tell me where else we might look for Jessie," he told Billy. "It's official. I'm back with the troopers and to stay."

"Hey—it's okay by me. Jessie won't mind. I mean, it's you, after all, right?"

"Right."

But he didn't know if that was true—official or not. Though Phil Becker had kept him up-to-date on what was going on in Jessie Arnold's life, Jensen had not communicated with her in six months' time. This was not because he hadn't wanted to, but because it was what she had said she preferred when he saw her last, in February, at the end of the long race from Whitehorse to Fairbanks. "I've never been good at dividing myself—can't live in two pieces," she had said when he had asked her to give it time so they could try to work it out. He had respected her decision, knowing their separation had been as difficult for her as it had been for him. "I love you" had been her very last words. And *that* he *did* know had been true.

Walking toward the new log house, he felt more than a little the intruder. He had lived with Jessie in the old one, felt at home there in a way he had discovered the hard way was impossible in Idaho. He smiled a little ruefully, remembering what his mother had told him less than a month earlier: "I think you'd better make up your mind to go north again, Alex, my boy. You're doing the part of yourself that's existing here no good at all." She had been right, as usual. But had he done himself any good by coming back to Alaska? That remained to be seen. And to see about it, he needed to see Jessie—who had disappeared. A dead man had been found at the fairground, where she was working, and now she was nowhere to be found. Were the two things related? He disliked coincidence.

Climbing the steps, he unlocked and opened the front door, stepped in, and closed it behind him. Without moving, he stood looking around. The space was larger than that of the old cabin, but still strangely familiar. As anticipated, the kitchen was in the back to the left, where it had been in the old cabin, with a big oak dining table nearby. The woodstove he remembered stood near the center of the room, as it had before. A different but comfortable sofa sat near it, piled with colorful pillows. A couple of easy chairs completed the friendly circle around the stove.

Where there had been a bedroom in the old cabin, there was now open space with a door to a bathroom that backed up to the kitchen. A wide window looked out into the woods to the rear of the lot, which allowed afternoon sunshine to pour in and gleam from the polished wood floor. Another easy chair and a reading lamp sat there under a stairway to a new upper level. The wall beside it had built-in shelves from top to bottom that were partially filled with books and a new music system.

The interior space felt empty, for it was very tidy and free of pictures on the walls and other memorabilia that Jessie had collected over the years—all destroyed in the fire, he knew. Hanging on the wall near the bathroom door was a rifle he recognized that had belonged to her father. A cast-iron dragon humidifier that puffed steam from its nostrils, now as cold as the woodstove on which it sat, had obviously been retrieved after the ashes cooled, and repainted, for the colors were subtly different.

The stairway led up to a loft, where he could see two doors, to what appeared to be a bedroom and an office. Slowly he crossed the room and went up, glancing into the office as he passed the first door, but continuing on to stand in the bedroom doorway. The brass bed it contained was not the one in which he remembered sleeping, but similar. It was spread with a quilt he recognized by its silver stars and northern lights. Jessie must have somehow snatched this favored thing from the fire. An open door in the bedroom led to another bath. It was larger than the one downstairs, painted white and accented with the cobalt blue that she loved. Seeing that it held a good-sized shower stall, he recalled bruises suffered from knocking his elbows on the hardware in the narrow confines of the one in the old cabin.

It seemed strange to be standing in Jessie's house without her. A book she had been reading was spread open, pages down, marking her place, on the bedside table. An oversized T-shirt of the kind in which she preferred to sleep hung on a hook on the wall. A flat bowl on a chest of drawers held a few pieces of jewelry and a colorful Iditarod pin. Reaching with one finger, Jensen separated a single diamond stud from the coils of a chain. He remembered giving her a pair for her birthday. One of them had been lost in the woods on an island in Kachemak Bay. He had promised her a replacement but had never got around to it.

Part of him felt voyeuristic and part quite at home. He left the bedroom and stood for a long minute on the balcony that ran the length of the house, looking down into the space below and attempting to reconcile those feelings. Giving up, he decided he should get to work. There would be time enough for resolutions when Jessie was back home where she belonged.

Jensen had gone back to the top of the stairs when he heard the rapid pounding of feet on the outside steps. He started down, intending to answer a knock that never came, for the door burst open and a man came hurriedly through it. Catching sight of Jensen halfway down, he stopped abruptly and stood staring up with a challenging frown.

"Ehlers?" Jensen asked. "Lynn Ehlers, I think."

"Where's Jessie?" Ehlers asked without responding to the query. "I hear she's got a dog missing. And what the hell are *you* doing in her house?"

CHAPTER 17

For a long minute Alex Jensen stared down at Lynn Ehlers, who stood just inside the door of Jessie's new log house. Then he continued his descent and ambled casually across the room to confront the man and his demand.

"I'm looking for some clue as to where she's gone," he said reasonably. "What are *you* doing in her house?"

Ehlers ignored the question. "I have a feeling she might not want you in here," he said. "You have no right to be going through her stuff. What do you mean, 'where she's gone'?"

For another minute Jensen let him wonder, while he wondered just how much to tell this man whom he considered a possible source of leads.

"We found her abandoned pickup out the Parks Highway, and she's disappeared," he said finally, watching closely for Ehlers's reaction to this bit of information.

"It's in the driveway," Ehlers stated flatly. "I just passed it on my way in."

"We brought it back to town."

"We?"

"Phil Becker and I. I'm back working with the Palmer troopers. You know Becker?"

"I know him. *So?* Where's Jessie?"

Jensen was not pleased by Ehlers's belligerent attitude, but held his temper. "We don't know that yet. Got any ideas?"

Ehlers thought for a minute. "Judy Clark says Tank's gone missing. She must be out looking for him."

"Without her truck?"

"Well, she can't have hiked off very far. She's got a bum knee. Did you check around where you found it?"

"Yes, and it had been sitting there for over four hours. Can you think of a reason she'd leave it that long?"

Ehlers shook his head and shrugged an unspoken negative response, the frown that creased his forehead changing to include worry along with hostility. Jensen's questions had put him on the defensive, which he found unwarranted.

The two men stood staring at each other in a confrontation they both knew had little to do with the subject at hand—and everything to do with Jessie Arnold personally.

Jensen finally broke the loaded silence. "How long has it been since you saw her?"

"Over a week. I stopped by to see if she needed anything from town, or help with the dogs she had kept here. But her knee's healed enough so she gets around okay on her own if she takes it easy."

"Sure you didn't see her earlier today?"

Ehlers fielded this insinuation with an elevation of temper. "No, dammit. Not today. Would I be here looking for her if I knew where she was? Just what the hell is this all about anyway? Seems like more than just a stolen dog to me."

"It is. A man's been murdered at the fairground in Palmer. Some of what we've learned about that may relate to a runaway boy and a blackmailing phone call Jessie got last night from whoever took Tank. She may not have gone off by choice."

The anger on Ehlers's face shifted to concern. "Oh, shit!" he said. Closing the door he had burst through, he crossed to the dining table near Jessie's kitchen and sat down heavily in one of her colorfully painted chairs. "Tell me. And what can I do to help? There's no sense wasting time circling each other like a pair of pit bulls."

So we both looked through the house for clues to where you might have been headed, but found nothing," Jensen explained. "Then Ehlers volunteered go back out to the kennel on Parks Highway where he was keeping his dogs—and yours, Jessie. He said he would gather some people there who were familiar with the area and begin a search for you. He left and I went to the office to meet Becker. But I went back later."

There's no way of telling where that threatening phone call was made," Becker told Jensen when he returned to the office. "There was no record of a call to Jessie's from a pay phone on the grounds. If Wease used a cell phone it must have belonged to someone else."

"Well, it was a long shot. Anything from Timmons at the lab?"

"Not much. The prints on the ax belong to the lumberjacks in the show, as we expected. I've got a man checking on all of them, but just to clear them. I don't expect anything really. We know the ax shouldn't have been left in the arena. They think it was somehow overlooked when they locked up the equipment they use twice a day. The shed where they're kept was still locked, with no sign of tampering. If it was left out, it could have been a lucky opportunity for the killer, not planned ahead of time. It may actually have inspired the killing.

"It's interesting, though, that Timmons says the dead guy was beat up pretty good before he was killed. Danny Tabor said that he saw two men arguing just before he took off on his bicycle that night. We know one of them was Wease, and I'm wondering if the other could have been Belmont. I didn't make anything of it when I talked to Danny because Wease interrupted before he could give me any details. But I think we'd better go have a chat with the boy in the morning. Let's concentrate on the other loose ends tonight. Knowing Jessie, she'll probably show up soon, wondering what all the fuss is about."

Jensen wasn't inclined to be so positive in his thinking. "Maybe," he said reluctantly. "Have to admit it wouldn't surprise me. But I'd be more comfortable if we knew where she is. If she doesn't show up—"

"Then we pull out all the stops. You find anything at her place?"

"Just Lynn Ehlers, with a defensive attitude until he found out she was missing. He's gone back out the road to do some more searching for her with a few friends." Jensen hesitated, then, "Has Ehlers been . . ." He stopped abruptly and swallowed the rest of the sentence.

"Been what?"

Jensen shook his head, changing his mind about whatever it was he was going to ask. "Nothing. It doesn't relate."

Becker waited a moment, considering the risk of answering the question he knew Jensen had been about to ask. "I don't know," he said finally. "But if you want me to speculate about Ehlers and Jessie—"

Jensen held up a restraining hand. "No, I don't want you to do that. I'll get an answer when it's appropriate—when we find Jessie. Until then it's not fair to put you, or anyone else, on the spot. It's my business—and hers. Let's leave it at that, okay?"

"Sure. If that's the way you want it."

"That's the way I want it. Now, what did the rest of those pictures have to tell us?"

Becker reached for the four envelopes containing the pictures from the film they had left to be developed. Opening them one by one, he took out the photos and laid each in a pile on the appropriate envelope. He laid the pictures that had been developed earlier and found in the red bag on another part of the desk.

"I looked these over again," he said, referring to the latter photos. "There's something we missed. Each one has a time of day penciled on the back."

Turning one over, he handed it to Jensen: "2:45 pm" was handwritten on the back.

"There's something else. I asked the photo shop to return the cartridges that contained the film for these new ones and to keep them with the pictures that had been in them. Each one of them has a time written on the side of it with a felt-tip pen—each one different."

He handed over one of the metal cartridges so Jensen could take a look at the writing.

"They were almost all taken at the same location, of the same area and building, at different times of day. When you put them in order of the times they were taken, they make an interesting, if rather enigmatic, sequence of people and things coming and going from that building. It gets even more interesting if you add in this last group of pictures we had developed. They're something else entirely."

He handed over the group to which he referred, then got up and moved around so he could watch over Jensen's shoulder as he examined them.

"The cartridge for these is labeled '8:45 am.' "

Jensen started through the pictures, tucking the one on top behind the others when he had seen it, keeping them in order. Reaching the fourth photo he stopped and, clearing a space on the front edge of Becker's desk, went back to the first, then laid them out in order across it.

The first photo showed an armored truck coming into the fairground through what was identifiable as the south gate, for the Chugach Mountains rose prominently in the background. A rear corner of the livestock barn was caught in the left-hand edge of the picture, and from the shadows it cast, it was easy to see that the image had been captured in the morning.

One by one, the photos followed the progression of the armored truck across the fairground and up to a red building on one side of the central plaza—the same building they had seen in the photos that had originally been found in the red bag. There the truck stopped, a door in the building opened, and two uniformed men got out and went inside. The next photo showed them coming out again carrying the canvas bags typically used to transfer deposits of cash from one secure location to another. In the last couple of pictures, the truck drove back across the plaza and out the gate through which it had entered the grounds.

Leaving the photos where he had placed them, Jensen leaned back in his chair and looked up at Becker. "I'd say there's more to this than just a stolen camera," he suggested.

"I'd say there could be a lot more," Becker agreed, returning to his chair behind the desk.

"I assume at least part of that building is where the day's cash is kept."

"Yes, but they don't publicize that fact. Very few people know exactly where it's secured at night—even people who work at the fair. Cash is collected from the ticket booths, and care is taken to disguise its transportation across the grounds to that location. Take a look at what the people going into that building are carrying in the pictures. It's never anything that looks like a money bag."

Jensen flipped through the photos again, identifying people and the burdens they carried—fast food sacks, boxes of frozen meat, a woman's large purse, an ordinary backpack. He nodded.

"This could put a whole new spin on Tank's disappearance—and Jessie's," Jensen said, scooping the photos back into a pile that preserved their order. "If this is what it appears to be, a plan for robbery, it explains Wease's motive for chasing the boy to get his camera bag back—also his reluctance to let you walk away with it and make the assumption you've just made. I think we'd better have another chat with your good buddy Wease, as well as Danny, don't you?"

"I do."

"Maybe even have the boy take a whack at identifying him?"

"My thought exactly. I've got to make a run into the crime lab with some stuff that can't wait on another case. I'll see if I can get any more information out of John Timmons while I'm there. You got a place to stay tonight, or do you want to crash with me?"

"Till I find a place to rent, I've got a space at the Lake Lucille Inn in Wasilla. You know—that Best Western by the lake where Caswell floats his plane sometimes?"

"Where he *used* to float it. You knew Cas crashed his plane this summer?"

"Yeah. I've got to call him, maybe tonight. How's he doing?"

"Good. Looking for another plane already."

Both men left the office, heading for the parking lot.

"Transportation?" Becker asked.

"I brought Jessie's truck back into town. Didn't think she'd mind. I left a note, but I'm going back out there anyway. She just might have turned up. Won't hurt to check on her dogs either, though Billy Steward was there earlier."

"Okay. If I get anything new I'll call you later," Becker promised, climbing into his own pickup. "Either at Lucille's or Jessie's."

Jensen watched him out of sight, then drove to Wasilla, where he stopped long enough to pick up a hamburger, onion rings, and a six-pack of Killian's before heading out the familiar eight miles on Knik Road. Half an hour later he was once again climbing the steps of Jessie's new house and letting himself in with the key that old Pete guarded in the dog yard.

CHAPTER 18

I had been at Jessie's long enough to finish eating and was headed for the sofa with a beer, to do some serious thinking, when I noticed that the answering machine was blinking," *Jensen told the group assembled in Jessie's living room.*

Several heads turned to glance at the table against the south wall, where the downstairs phone resided, but the machine was not blinking at the moment.

"It reminded me that I meant to call Caswell, but I thought I'd better find out what was on the tape. It could have been another message from the dog-napper."

Frank Monroe couldn't help smiling at the word Alex had jury-rigged.

"But it wasn't, was it?" Jessie asked.

"No. It was someone named Maxie, checking in from the Yukon Territories. From the message, I assumed it was your

friend from the night before. She left her cell phone number, so I called her back, thinking she might shed some light on where you'd gone that morning."

"Maxie," a husky voice answered on the second ring.

"You don't know me. I'm Alex Jensen. I'm calling on behalf of—"

"I know who you are," Maxie interrupted. "You're Jessie's Alex—one of the boys in blue."

"State trooper, actually. Look, I got the message you left on Jessie's machine. You were here last night, right?"

"That's right. Where's Jessie?"

"Could you tell me where you are now?"

"Question with a question. Sounds official. I made very good time and drove late. I'm at Kluane Lake until tomorrow morning. Is something wrong, Alex? Where's Jessie?"

"We're not sure. We found her truck out the Parks Highway, but she hasn't been seen since this morning."

"Beg yours?"

"Excuse me?"

"You said she's missing?"

"Yes—never made it in to work at the fair today."

"Bloody hell!" Maxie's voice came sharply back, apprehensive and frustrated. "I warned her that going hunting for Tank was a crook idea. But it doesn't surprise me that she went anyway. She did, didn't she?"

"We think so. Do you have any idea exactly where?"

"No. I wish I did. If I hadn't promised to be in Colorado yesterday, I'd turn around and come right back there."

There was a long moment of silence, then Maxie spoke again. "Please, will you keep me posted until you find her?"

"Of course. This number?"

"Yes, in the evening I'm usually someplace where this cell thing works. If you don't mind my asking—oh hell, even if you do. What are you doing back in Alaska?"

"Well-l," Jensen practically stuttered in surprise that this stranger would ask, or know anything about him, "that's a long story."

"I'm a forward and practical woman," Maxie gave him to understand. "You're permanently back?"

"Yes."

"Good. Does she know?"

"Not yet."

"But you intend that she should?"

"Yes."

"Okay. That's enough of your business. How can I reach you if I think of anything valuable? But she didn't tell me anything really."

He gave her the number of the Palmer office, and before she hung up, she promised to keep in touch. Then she was gone; leaving him staring at the phone in his hand, dazed and a little abashed. She had made straightening out his relationship with Jessie seem simple in a way. He dropped the receiver back in its cradle and went back to sit down on the sofa and finish the beer he had carted along to the phone.

Feeling jet-lagged, he leaned back on a pile of pillows and

slowly emptied the bottle, trying to concentrate on prioritizing the events of the last twenty-four hours.

I had meant to leave a note and go back to the Lake Lucille Inn, but the next thing I knew there was sunshine coming in the window and I'd spent the night on your sofa," he told Jessie across the circle. "Some time in between I'd kicked off my boots and rolled up in an afghan. I came to when Becker started hammering on the front door."

Still half asleep, Jensen had stumbled to his feet to answer the knock. "Oh, it's you. Thought it might be—"

"Nope. But I thought I'd find you here," Becker said as a bleary-eyed Jensen stood in his stocking feet holding the door open and gathering his wits.

"I crashed and burned last night. Bedtime comes two hours earlier in Idaho, and I didn't get much sleep in the Seattle airport yesterday."

"When you weren't at the Lake Lucille Inn, I hoped Jessie had come home from—wherever."

"No. Make some coffee while I take a quick shower, will you?"

"Sure."

As Becker headed for the kitchen, Jensen climbed the stairs to Jessie's bedroom, where he stripped off his clothes and climbed into her new shower. A welcome cascade of hot water helped bring him back to life. The mug of strong coffee Becker handed him when he came back down ten minutes later completed the job.

"Time to interrogate Wease?" he asked, retrieving his pipe and joining Becker, who was drinking his own coffee at the dining table. "Then we'll talk to the boy?"

"It's what I had in mind." Becker nodded and watched as Jensen lit the pipe with a kitchen match. "Why don't you get one of those special lighters for pipes?"

"Tried 'em. They don't work as well as matches. Besides, I've always kind of enjoyed the smell of sulfur. Reminds me of lighting the woodstove when I was a kid at home."

He frowned in concentration and began to think out loud. "It seems to me that we should really dig into this guy Wease. In thinking it over, it seems to me that he's probably our best bet for finding out what's going on here, both with Jessie and with what looks like a crime in the planning stages, if not in progress. If we push him hard enough it should . . ."

As he continued to lay out what he had come up with since talking to Becker the night before, he flipped his hand to extinguish the match, then held it hesitantly for a moment, realizing he had no place to put it down. Still talking, he casually got up and walked into the kitchen, where he opened a cupboard above the stove, extracted an ashtray that he obviously expected to find there, and returned. Setting it on the table, he dropped the burned match into it.

Becker watched the maneuver with an interest in how subconsciously Jensen was making himself at home in Jessie's living space, but said nothing to break into the other man's verbal analysis of what should be done about Ron Wease. The ease of the activity he had just observed revealed everything about Jensen's aspirations for the relationship, but calling attention to that would serve nothing, so once again Becker simply noted and mentally filed it.

"We'll head for the fairground first," he said when Jensen finished talking. "It'll be faster to find Wease's address through Dave Lomax at the security office, if he's not off somewhere on the grounds."

But Ron Wease was not to be found on the grounds.

"Never showed up today," the director of security for the fair, Dave Lomax, told them angrily. "No phone call or nothin'. He's history. I've already replaced him."

"That's a pretty knee-jerk response, isn't it?" Jensen asked. "How do you know for sure he won't show up?"

"Well"—Lomax scowled—"I guess I don't. But it's not the first time. I gotta have dependable people, so I'm done putting up with—"

"You got an address? Even better, a picture on his records?" Becker broke in.

"I can give you a home address and phone number, but no photo."

"Well, we know what he looks like anyway, but I thought photos were part of your security records."

"Yeah—we take our own with a Polaroid. He kept saying he'd get it done but never seemed to get around to it."

Lomax sorted through a file in the drawer of his desk and came up with an application form that he handed to Becker. "See—no picture."

With a scowl, Becker copied down the address listed. "Sloppy," he growled, which earned him a speculative and resentful glare from Lomax as the two troopers went out the door.

"You know," Jensen said as they headed for the address Ron Wease had given on his application form, "there's one thing that bothers me about all this that we haven't talked about."

"What's that?"

"The boy, Danny whatsisname, saw Wease behind the pub that night arguing with someone. I keep wondering if that someone could have been Belmont. If it was, there could have been more to their disagreement than an argument. Wease chased the boy, but he could have come back later to beat up on Belmont and wound up killing him. I want to know what that *argument* was about."

"Tabor—the boy's name. And it's possible, I guess. Wease interrupted my conversation with Danny, so I didn't ask if the argument involved Belmont. I think we should talk to both of them again—probably the old man, too."

"Let's find Wease first."

They found him, but there would be no interrogation. The dead don't answer questions. Whatever Ron Wease had known, if anything, he would not be telling them—or anyone else.

The door to his efficiency apartment was unlocked and partially open when the two officers climbed a flight of battered stairs to the second floor of a South Palmer eight-plex unit in need of a paint job. Wease was sprawled facedown in the narrow space that served as his kitchen on one side of the room. The butcher knife that had been used to slit his throat lay beside him on the ancient tile floor that was now a murderous abstract in red and gray-green.

"God dammit!" Becker exclaimed in frustration and disgust as he used his phone to begin the process that would bring a crime lab team, probably with John Timmons in tow.

It was much later before they were able to return to the idea of talking to Danny Tabor again.

Too much later, as it turned out.

CHAPTER 19

Why was it too late?" John Timmons asked. "I never heard this part."

"When you and the team from the lab got to Wease to take over, we went looking for Danny," Becker explained. "But he wasn't at home where he was supposed to be. Just his parents were there, upset and confused. His mother had left him doing yard work to go to the grocery, and when she came back he was gone. You tell it, Danny. It happened to you, after all."

Danny yawned and sat up from where he had been leaning a bit sleepily against Jessie's good leg.

"Yeah, it sure did. I didn't remember seeing that guy before, and he was scarier than the other one. Besides, I thought my dad would never understand why I left. If that man hadn't showed up I wouldn't have—but when he did, I just had to."

• • •

Doug Tabor had roused his son, Danny, at six o'clock that morning, when he and his wife got up for the day, though he was normally allowed to sleep until at least seven. The family ate breakfast together, then Doug and Danny went to the garage and sorted out the tools the boy would need for the jobs he had been assigned.

"I'll be home for lunch," his father told him. "And you'd better have a lot of yard work accomplished by then—at least the lawn mowed and a good start on the edging. Got it?"

Danny nodded, his focus on the rake he was twisting in one hand.

"Look at me when I talk to you," Doug demanded. "It's a very narrow line you're walking here."

"Yes, sir," Danny agreed, presenting a serious face to his father.

"Good. Now get busy."

By ten o'clock the lawn was mowed, and Danny was busy with the rake when Jill Tabor came out the front door, purse and car keys in hand, pausing on her way to the garage.

"I'm going to the grocery store," she told him. "I won't be gone long. There's a peanut butter and jelly sandwich and some orange juice on the kitchen counter. Take a quick break, then get back to it, okay?"

Still holding the rake, he crossed to where she stood on the front walk. "Thanks, Mom," he said with a smile.

She reached to lay a hand on his shoulder. "You're doing a good job, Danny."

"Thanks."

Continuing to the garage, she raised the door and backed

the car out, leaving the door open. Danny could see his bicycle just inside, where his father had stashed it—off-limits as long as he was grounded.

When she had driven away, he went inside to claim his reward and took the food back outside, where he sat down on the front step to eat it, beside the rake he had dropped there. The peanut butter was crunchy, his favorite. While he chewed, he thought about the elephant ears he and Mr. Monroe had eaten for breakfast at the fair and decided he liked the sandwich better and that his mom must not be so mad at him now.

A whole month of being grounded would be a long time, but he knew his father hadn't been unfair in setting it. Had it been worth it? He thought it had. The old man had been a lot of fun, really. A grin spread across his face as he remembered being a scarecrow and how the goat had jumped and bleated when Mr. Monroe poked it with his cane. The grin faded as he thought about talking to Jessie about being responsible enough to earn a dog of his own. He guessed he probably wouldn't be able to start counting good behavior until his month of being grounded was over.

As he daydreamed of playing with a dog, the sound of a vehicle intruded, and he looked up to see a pickup driving up the street. In front of his house, it slowed. The window was down on the driver's side, and the driver, a man wearing a baseball cap and sunglasses whom Danny didn't recognize, gave him and the empty garage a long look. Though the sunglasses weren't the reflective kind, they reminded Danny unpleasantly of the man who had chased him at the fairground.

The way the man in the truck was staring made him uneasy as well.

Then the pickup stopped completely, and the driver leaned his head out. "Hey, kid," he called. "Do you know where Pioneer Street is?"

Stuffing the last bite of sandwich into his mouth, Danny raised an arm and pointed down the street.

"Where? I've been down there and couldn't find it."

Danny chewed and swallowed. "Two blocks," he called.

"Do you know if the Jordans live down there?"

"No," said Danny, picking up the glass of orange juice.

"What?"

"No, I don't," a little louder this time and followed by a sip of juice. He wished the man would go away.

"I can't hear you." The man put the gears in park, opened the door, and stepped out onto the street, leaving the engine running. He trotted swiftly up the walk toward Danny. "What did you say?"

The speed at which he came alarmed the boy, who jumped up and dropped the half-empty glass of orange juice, which broke on the cement walk. One step back brought him up against the front door, but there wasn't time to open it and escape into the house.

The man lunged at him, hands outstretched to grab, and Danny dodged under the one on his right, left footprints in his mother's flower bed, and leaped onto the lawn. The man spun around and came after him, but the boy was already halfway to the garage. Seizing his bicycle, he threw himself onto it and pedaled away down the drive. Determined fingers plucked at his shirttail, but lost their hold and slid ineffectually away as he accelerated. He could hear swearing behind him as he swerved into the road, then, almost immediately, came the sound of the engine's roar as the driver turned the pickup around in a rattle of flying gravel.

By the time it was speeding after Danny, he had left the road, fleeing between two neighbors' houses, and was riding hard across the same vacant lot he had traversed in running away from home the first time.

"You are not to leave the yard without permission," he remembered his father's dictate of the night before.

A month might be nothing compared to the punishment that would be forthcoming when his mother came home and found him gone again. *I'll be grounded for the rest of my life,* he thought, but didn't know what else he could have done.

Who was this guy anyway, and what did he want? It couldn't be the bag. They'd given that to the police, hadn't they?

Reaching the next street, which ran parallel to his own, he glanced to the left and saw the pickup turn the corner, coming in his direction in a hurry. But riding bicycles with his friends had given Danny firsthand knowledge of the shortcuts in the neighborhood. He rode straight across the street, up a driveway, and into another vacant lot. Halfway across it, the path he was following turned abruptly down an embankment toward a road at a lower level. Going too fast, he sailed over the edge and was airborne for several yards before hitting the packed ground at the bottom. The bicycle tilted dangerously, but he managed to right it and allowed the momentum to carry him over several rolling hillocks that were easy to ride at a lower speed but jarred his teeth in the struggle to keep from crashing the bouncing bike. Coasting out onto the road, he followed it in a wide curve until, some distance behind him, he could hear the roar of the pickup engine, coming fast.

Abandoning the road again, he swung into another driveway, past a house, and into a backyard where a woman was sitting at a picnic table reading a newspaper.

"Hey!" she shouted. But anything else she said was blown away in the breeze of his passing.

Another street, this one a dead end with a barrier, around which Danny swerved. Pedaling frantically on, he tried to think where to go so the threatening stranger in the truck couldn't find him. There had to be somewhere—and someone who would help.

Then suddenly he knew exactly who to find—someone who already knew all about it. Maybe on the way he could lose the man in the pickup that he could still faintly hear somewhere out of sight.

And you came home to an empty house and yard?" Timmons turned to Jill Tabor.

"Yes. I saw the broken glass on the front walk, and at first I thought maybe he was in the house, getting something to clean it up. I took the groceries inside and called, but he wasn't there. When I went back out I noticed that his bicycle was gone, and I knew he wasn't supposed to be riding it. Doug was due home for lunch, and I knew he'd be furious, but there wasn't much I could

do. I thought about going to look for Danny in the car, but I had no idea where to go—which direction he'd gone. I couldn't understand why he would take off again. He's a good kid, and it didn't make sense."

"So you came home and were *furious?"*

"I sure was,*" Doug Tabor affirmed. "I thought he was being obstinate and playing some game again, though I had to agree that it didn't seem like Danny. Jill said he'd been working hard all morning and that broken glass worried both of us."*

"What did you do?"

"I got back on the road and drove around the neighborhood looking for him—asking if anyone I knew had seen him. That was when April Shepherd—she lives a couple of streets over—said that he'd streaked through her yard on his bicycle less than an hour earlier like a bat out of hell and looking scared. That's when we decided to call the police."

"We didn't get the word until we showed up thinking we'd find Danny at home and instead ran into a couple of worried parents," Jensen said. "So another APB went out for Danny. But after finding Wease dead, we had other things on our minds. And there was growing concern for Jessie because it was then that Lynn Ehlers's call came in from out the road."

CHAPTER 20

In a wilderness cabin, far from anything familiar, Jessie Arnold sat on the floor where she had been for a day, a night, and most of another day.

The ramshackle cabin exhibited evidence of having been abandoned for years, long enough for the low sod roof to collapse in one rear corner and a ragged hole or two in the rest to give it a decidedly unstable appearance, though the horizontal beams and rafters appeared strong. The small amount of light that fell through the holes in the roof and inadequate windows had allowed Jessie to study a fraction of the walls, floor, and disintegrating ceiling. She would have given anything to be able to examine it all more closely—better still, to free Tank and walk out of the trap in which she had spent the last day and a half. But it seemed that, with precision and shrewdness, her captor had anticipated every escape she might possibly attempt and had obstructed it by the very nature of her imprisonment.

From where she sat on the floor, she could see through the narrow windows, empty of all but a few fragments of glass, that spruce trees surrounded the cabin. Although it was the end of August and the sun was lower than it had been in June, their thick branches prevented light from finding its way in, and the interior of the ancient building was damp and chilly. The dusty tattered lace of small spiders clung in the corners and between the logs where chinking had long ago fallen away, leaving gaps up to an inch wide. The scent of moldering wood hung in the air like an invisible fog, reminding her how improbable it was that anyone would think to look for her in this evidently remote location.

A chain padlocked around Jessie's wrists held her arms and shoulders, aching with cramp, over her head. Her hands felt as if they were made of ice, and the fingers of the right, with which she kept a grip on the chain, were numb. Soon she would have to stand up again in order to lower them for a few minutes' ease, though she knew she must take care to keep tension on the chain in doing so. It was not a heavy chain. A pair of bolt cutters would have severed it. But the lack of such a tool made it as effective as one much more massive and stout. Her abductor must have considered that links of larger size could hang up on the rafters above, allowing relief, or escape, and had used the smallest size necessary to assure her confinement and continued attention. Not for the first time she examined the line of links that went up from her wrists to the beam overhead. From there it hung horizontally across the gap between it and another such beam, then went down and was securely fastened to the nearby platform that, with tension on the chain, she was attempting to keep level.

Attention and alertness were imperative given the circumstances. She was tired, and with nothing to do but wait, she was more than a little afraid she would fall asleep and fail to keep the chain at the essential tautness. She was also thirsty and so hungry she felt slightly sick.

Her head ached from the unexpected blow that had knocked her unconscious before she could see who had slipped up without her notice to deliver it. But she remembered standing by a shed in a wretched and unfamiliar dog yard near the Parks Highway north of Wasilla, visually checking each of the dogs tethered with similar chains to iron stakes driven into the ground next to their dilapidated boxes. She recalled with disgust that the unkempt kennel had been ripe with the filthy odor of more than twenty canines existing in the squalor of their own waste. Though she was used to the barks and yelps of her own dogs if a stranger entered their yard, these had lunged against the restraint of their chains, howling, baying, and baring their fangs in savage snarls, some crouched to spring if given an opportunity to reach her. Jessie had noticed they were thin to the point of emaciation, several bearing scars from fights and beatings, when she heard someone move close behind her.

She remembered nothing until later, when she became aware of some kind of plastic covering her. She was bound so tightly she could only lie helpless, facedown on a vibrating metal surface. It wasn't hard to deduce that she was in the back of a pickup truck in motion. But there was no way to figure out why, who was driving, or where they were headed. She had no way of knowing where she was, or how long the drive had been before she came to, but her head ached, and she longed for the vibration to stop. Considering the silencing tape that covered her mouth, her main objective was to focus enough willpower to keep from throwing up against it. Then she passed out again and woke in the cabin with a blindfold covering her eyes, but the tape that had covered her mouth was gone.

"You feel this?" a rough whisper had said in her ear. She felt a jerk on the chain that held her wrists over her head, heard and felt it vibrate with tension. "You'll be sorry if you don't keep it tight. Don't move or you'll be very, very sorry. You can get that off your eyes when you hear the door shut. Understand?"

Dizzy and bewildered, she nodded and sat still, feeling the tension of the chain.

"Answer me," the whisper demanded. It was a faintly familiar whisper, but dizzy and sick, she hadn't been able to think where she had heard it before—or if she actually had.

"Yes. I understand."

Footsteps crossed the room. Then she heard the squeal of protest from metal hinges and the thud of a wooden door closing.

For a minute or two Jessie remained where she was without moving. There had been threat in that voice, and she had no way of knowing what it meant. It would be best, she decided, to move as little as possible until she could see and assess the situation. Carefully keeping the chain taut, she rubbed one side of her face against her outstretched arm, and the blindfold, a loosely tied piece of dark fabric with ragged edges, fell away more easily than she expected. Slowly her eyes adjusted to the dim light. At first she was confused by what she was seeing. Then, as she appraised her position and what it meant, fear and anger followed swiftly.

Now, taking a deep breath, Jessie refused to think about it anymore. Slowly, cautiously, she began the harrowing process of getting to her feet. Intent on not allowing even one link of the chain to slip against the wooden beam, she kept her wrists at a constant height from the floor as she straightened her legs. With great care, she raised herself until she was finally upright, and her wrists now maintained the chain's tension at waist level. The motion resulted in a sharp complaint from the knee she had injured earlier in the summer, and the pain in her arms, neck, and shoulders increased with the motion, then subsided slowly into more tolerable aches. Hooking her thumbs into the belt loops of her jeans, she held the chain steady and alternately rotated her shoulders in small circles against the hurt. Though the motion was guarded, one link made a metallic click as it slid across the beam. Immediately Jessie increased the tension on the chain until that single link slid back in her direction.

Across the room, Tank, awakened by the small jerk and click of the moving chain, raised his head to look across at her. Seeing his mistress standing up, he waved his tail and started to pull his legs up under him, plainly intending to get up as well.

"No!" Jessie said sharply. Her dry voice cracked, but fearful, she ignored it. "Lie down, good boy. *Lie down.*"

He cocked his head but relaxed and stayed where he was, six feet above the floor, watching closely to see if this time she was inclined to action and to leaving this place. But he obeyed her command and continued to lie still as she insisted. He lay on a four-foot-square rectangle of ancient plywood that rested horizontally, one end supported by a single, tall sawhorse, the other by the chain that was nailed to it, which Jessie supported with opposing tension.

Fastened with a slipknot around his neck was a yellow nylon cord, flexible and perhaps a quarter of an inch thick. The length of it was tied to the overhead beam with only a few precious inches of slack that were not enough to allow the dog to reach the floor. If he attempted to jump from his plywood platform, the cord would tighten relentlessly and he would hang suspended until he strangled. If Jessie failed to maintain the tension on the chain that kept it level, or tightened it so it tipped the platform in the other direction, he would slide off. If any of these things happened, restrained by the chain and the weight of the plywood attached to the other end, she would be unable to cross the room in time to save him. As had been clearly planned by her abductor, this knowledge had kept her all but motionless as the long hours passed. She was frustrated and tense, but still searched for a solution to the situation—a way out of the trap that had been so cleverly and effectively designed.

"Good boy," she crooned to her dog. "Be still. I know you're as hungry and thirsty as I am, but you're a good dog to stay—a very good dog. It's okay. We're okay, you and me, and I won't let anything bad happen."

Inactivity was difficult for an active animal. Unaware of his peril but increasingly restless and tired of staying where he was, Tank whined softly, but once again obeyed and laid his muzzle back down on his forepaws.

Gingerly, Jessie raised her knees alternately toward her chest, working them to alleviate tired muscles. She was cautious with the injured one, bringing it up only until a twinge of pain warned her to stop, then lowering it again. There was no way to sit on the hard wooden floor that did not result in discomfort, and as it was impossible to lie down, her whole body protested the punishment. Straightening her back, she rolled her head, then brought her chin down to touch her chest, trying to relieve the strain in her shoulders and neck. It helped a little, but not much.

In fact, nothing helped much. And time, she knew, would only make it worse. Slowly, carefully, she sat back down, forced to adjust once more to the pain that tension created in her arms. She tried again to think who could have brought her here—and why. She remembered standing in an unfamiliar dog yard, but little after that. Why was she confined here so carefully? The arrangement seemed to indicate prior planning, but how could her abductor have known where she would be? What did he want? And when would he come back? Or would he?

Turning a little to the right, she looked out the small square of empty window into the shadows of the dark spruce outside. A ray or two of early evening sunlight glimmered through the thick branches as a breeze set them waving gently. A bedraggled spiderweb hanging in the window frame was momentarily caught and gilded in one narrow beam of light.

Jessie sighed in discouragement. It would eventually grow dark and there would be another night to endure. The hours of the night had been the worst, for the dark had prevented her from seeing across the room to her dog. She had only been able to speak encouragingly to him now and then and hope that he would stay where he was. She had been able to hear him shift position, which he had done several times, but not being able to reassure herself visually that he was safe had been a nightmare of stress.

Don't think about it now, she told herself, turning back to look toward him again. *Think of a way to get us both out of here.*

Her arms, shoulders, and back were now on fire with cramp and strain. She could not feel her hands. But she stubbornly refused to permit the chain that held the platform on which her lead dog rested to slip and tip him off to strangle. Her whole body protested the ill treatment, and lack of sleep was making it increasingly hard for her to concentrate.

The dog lay, listless and still, where she had ceaselessly encouraged him to stay. He was such a good dog. Any other would long ago have refused to obey commands and tried to jump down, throttling itself in the process. She knew he was as hungry and thirsty as she was, and she was amazed at his capacity for compliance in the face of such punishment. Her stomach had burned with ravenous complaints, but now she only felt light-headed. How much longer could it last? How much longer could *she* last?

As she shifted position slightly, Tank lifted his head in her direction.

"Stay," she tried to say, but her word came out as a croak, forcing her to clear her throat in order to be even hoarsely understandable. "Please stay, good puppy."

Once again his muzzle dropped wearily back onto his paws, though his eyes never left her. Somehow he seemed to know how important it was to do her bidding. At some time during the long hours of captivity, she had noticed that he was no longer wearing his new orange bandana and had wondered where it had gone.

Her view of Tank and the room swam in sudden helpless tears and she was overwhelmed with the knowledge that she had never loved this dog so much, needed so much not to lose him, or felt so helpless. Tears that she was unable to wipe away ran down her face. Would this never end? Would no one ever come? Was this what her captor had intended all along; that she would watch her favorite dog die out here, before she died herself? The diabolical cruelty of the situation roused her anger again, which was marginally strengthening because it roused her determination as well.

Calculating the risk, she had tried once to free the two of them and almost lost Tank in the process. Earlier that afternoon, knowing her strength was failing and that she would soon be physically unable to make an attempt, she had tried to jump high enough to reach the beam above her. She had reached it with the fingers of one hand and clung perilously, catching the chain under her fingers to keep it from slipping away. But it had proved impossible to hold on or to pull herself up.

Keeping tight hold on the chain alone, she had been forced to allow herself to slide back to the floor, landing hard on the leg with the injured knee, which had left her gasping in pain as it collapsed under her. The resulting jerk had almost tipped the dog from his precarious perch on the plywood platform, but Jessie had clung tenaciously and righted the situation by sliding a few links back over the beam in his direction.

There was still a throb of pain in the knee, which turned to flame with any motion, and she could only hope she had not ruined the surgery performed earlier that summer. But even that didn't seem to matter much. Only one thing was important: maintaining the status quo.

Briefly she wondered what Joanne had thought when she didn't appear as planned to help out at the Iditarod booth. Had Maxie called, as promised, and left a message in an empty house for no one to hear? She thought that perhaps tomorrow, after two nights with no answer, her friend might call the troopers to let them know she hadn't been able to reach Jessie. That, she decided, was probably wishful thinking. Maxie would leave at least two or three messages before becoming seriously concerned. What would Becker think when he couldn't find her and wanted to know more about the phone call? She was glad now that she had called him, but didn't see how it would help anyone find her. Would someone notice that her truck had been abandoned and wonder why she hadn't returned?

It was hard to focus—easier just to wait and try to rest, reserving any remaining energy for the task at hand. Nothing else mattered.

Jessie stared across the room at the shattered window. A tiny spider crawled out onto a web it had spun between the frame and a shard of broken glass. It reached a small fly that had been unlucky enough to become stranded on a sticky thread and began to restrict its struggles by encasing it in a silk shroud, skillfully turning it over and over. A breath of breeze caused the web and its passengers to shiver, but the spider took no notice, continuing its task until the fly hung motionless, its fate secured.

Where was the inhuman spider who had spun this web of chain on which she and her lead dog hung powerless? Jessie wondered. Who was he, and would he return to seal their fate as well?

CHAPTER 21

"What did Lynn say when he called?" she asked Jensen now, leaning forward in her seat on the sofa.

"He and several others had been looking for you until dark the night before," he told her. "You've got a lot of friends out there, Jess. When it got dark and they'd come up empty, they went back out the next morning. Six of them went in pairs. One pair drove to Talkeetna, where they found that no one had seen you, and started back, searching every road and trail as they came. Another pair went to Houston and started searching between there and Nancy Lake. Ehlers and the musher he's staying with were working the roads and kennels northwest of Nancy Lake.

"For most of the morning they found nothing. Then, on one of the roads that ended in a trail too narrow for their truck, they

found a blue plastic five-gallon water container with 'Arnold' written on it with black felt-tip marker."

"That was in the back of my pickup," Jessie said with a confused frown. "But they didn't find it on the same road where you found my truck, did they?"

"No. It was on one a few miles farther toward Talkeetna. From what we can figure out now, he transported you—from where he hit you to the location where Ehlers found the water can—in your own pickup. I don't see any other way your tire tracks could have wound up in the mud at the side of that road. And they were there. After leaving you in that cabin, he must have driven your pickup back to where it was found, then hiked back for his own. That road by the trail was rough and full of potholes, several right there where he stopped. The can was empty and must have bounced out. Evidently he didn't notice. Your name wasn't visible until Ehlers turned it over. Then he left it and found a phone to call us."

"Thank God he didn't assume it was trash," Jessie sighed.

"Just after Ehlers called, your call came in, Frank," Becker said, turning to Monroe. "We were already headed out the road, having left Danny's parents with the assurance that all our resources were aware of his disappearance and looking for him."

"Correct." Monroe nodded agreement. "That's when Danny appeared on his bicycle."

Frank Monroe, neatly dressed, sat on a bench outside the Palmer Senior Center for Assisted Living so he could smoke his pipe while he worked. With care and resolution, he was going through the newspaper's list of advertisements for apartment rentals in downtown Palmer and circling any that interested him with a red pencil.

For the most part the staff of the senior center had treated him in a respectful, if cautious, fashion since his return from his brief vacation, though some of them, Nurse Doris Richards in particular, had tried to pretend he hadn't returned at all and assiduously ignored him. No one had entered his room without knocking, not even the housekeeper. The nurse's aide had gone so far as to put a flower on his breakfast tray rather than complain because he wasn't eating in the dining room.

The administrator had passed him twice that morning with a resentful frown, but he expected nothing less. She was clearly angry, but his attorney would take care of that. The attorney had dropped in on his way to the office to have a long talk with Frank Monroe, to ascertain his wishes before approaching the administrator, and had assured him that he had nothing to worry about contractually with the institution.

"They can't have things both ways," he had stated categorically. "By contract, they were responsible for you. What makes this easier is that they allowed you to slip away for more than twenty-four hours without informing law enforcement or your nephew. We can, and will, threaten legal action over that if they refuse to refund a reasonable amount of your money. Don't worry about it. They'll be glad to come to a realistic agreement. You'll be fine."

Neither the solicitous nor the disapproving treatment within the walls of the center bothered Monroe in the slightest. He was cheerfully eager to start rearranging his life to suit himself. He had just circled the last interesting ad in the paper when the sound of swiftly approaching tires on the circular driveway in front of the senior center attracted his attention. Looking up, he was startled to see Danny Tabor swing himself off his bicycle and wheel it rapidly up the walk toward where his friend sat on the bench.

The boy was panting with the exertion of pedaling. Sweat stood out on his face, and his T-shirt was damp with it. Eyes wide with alarm, he began to spill out words between gasps faster than Monroe could completely understand, but it was clear that he was frightened.

"There's a guy—after me—in a pickup truck—tried to grab me, but—I got away. He's coming—I gotta hide—"

"Danny. *Danny*. Slow down. Stop and slow down. I can't understand. Who's *after you*? The guy from the fair?"

"No. Some other guy in a truck. Help me. Hide me before—"

He was interrupted by the sound of a vehicle on the circular driveway. They both turned their heads to see a pickup coming toward them.

"That's *him*," Danny piped, his voice high with fear. "O-oh, I gotta get away." He shoved his bicycle to the open front door of the senior center and vanished into the lobby.

With the distraction of two things in motion, Frank Monroe didn't have the opportunity to get more than a glancing impression of the driver or of the pickup, which did not stop but continued on around the driveway and back out into the street, where it sped away. Aside from the fact that it was brown and white, he had no idea of the make or model, nor did he have a chance to read the license plate number. It came and went too fast and was gone as he was rising to his feet.

Dropping the newspaper on the bench, he went into the center, where he found Danny being confronted by the angry administrator.

"You can't bring that bicycle in here," she was admonishing the boy. "Take it back outside where it belongs. *Immediately.*"

"But—but—" Danny was trying to explain.

"Here now," Monroe told the administrator. "Leave the boy alone. He's a friend of mine."

"Well, I should have known." She whirled and stalked back in the direction of her office.

"Is he still out there?" Danny asked.

"No. He's gone. Bring your bicycle over here by the door and lean it against the wall where it's out of the way. No one will bother it. *Right?*"

He aimed the question at the administrator, who he could see was watching from inside her office, and allowed himself a smile of satisfaction when she sharply shut the door.

"Come with me, Danny." He laid a hand on the boy's shoulder and guided him down the hall toward his *pigeonhole.* "You're safe here with me. You can tell me all about it, and we'll figure out what to do."

CHAPTER 22

The radio in Becker's pickup crackled to life as he and Jensen sped up a hill on the far side of Wasilla, heading out the Parks Highway to where Ehlers said they had found the water container that bore Jessie's name. In a quick exchange, the dispatcher relayed information from Frank Monroe that Danny Tabor was with him at the senior center and that someone had chased him there in a pickup truck. Becker told them to call his parents and to make sure both the boy and the old man were safe and taken care of until he could make it back to Palmer to talk to them.

"We sent a patrol car," the dispatcher responded. "The parents are on the way."

"Good. Be sure someone keeps track of the two of them. It's important."

He concentrated on his driving for a minute or two before breaking the silence.

"Exactly how the hell is all this connected?" he asked Jensen finally, gnawing at his lower lip in frustration. "There's so much going on at once that it's hard to get a handle on how it fits together."

"We don't have all the pieces," Jensen stated flatly. "There's one very large one missing—who else is involved? We've got two dead men. Wease, who I'm willing to bet killed Belmont—if we're right, the boy can identify him as the person who was fighting with Belmont that night. But someone else killed Wease. Who and why? The best I can come up with is a falling out of some kind among thieves. The fact that the boy and the old man are the only two that may be able to put the two of them together doesn't seem to matter with both of them dead. Someone else was chasing Danny Tabor this time. Who? At a guess, it might be the person who killed Wease. But why? The boy couldn't have witnessed that. Going after the boy indicates a degree of desperation over something we don't know about. The thing that makes most sense is that one of them, or both, saw or knows something significant, or this someone thinks they do. If they do, they may not even realize they know it."

"It's possible that whoever it is doesn't know that we developed the photos of the armored car and are onto this robbery idea," Becker speculated. "An alternative is that he doesn't know I even have the bag and thinks Danny or Frank Monroe still has the bag, film, and photos and is trying to get them back."

"Either of those things is imaginable. There are several things that do relate in all this. Danny had the bag. Whoever stole Jessie's dog wanted that bag. Wease chased Danny because he said the bag was his and he wanted it badly. So he may have been Jessie's threatening caller. Jessie went looking for Tank and vanished. Wease may have been responsible for both disappearances before he was killed. But he was a security guard at the fair, with a schedule to keep and people like Dave Lomax who would notice if he was absent for any significant amount of time. Lomax did say it wasn't the first time Wease had missed work. I wish we'd asked him exactly when and for how long Wease wasn't where he was supposed to be.

"What I can't get hold of is just how the two locations—the fairground and out here somewhere—fit together. The area out here on the Parks Highway is where Jessie obviously came looking for Tank, but only on a hunch about where he might be most easily hidden. According to that friend of hers, Maxie, it was just an idea. She didn't *know* he was here.

"The whole thing with the boy and Monroe took place at the fairground. Tank was taken from the fairground, and Belmont was found there. There has to be someone involved besides Wease who knew everything that was going on. So maybe this someone who's there a lot works there, or volunteers, like Jessie. It took more than a few minutes to remove Tank from the fair to wherever he was taken. If it's a worker at the fair, someone may have noticed that whoever took him was gone for that vital amount of time. One person can't be in two places at once, can they? Of course, there may be more than one." He shrugged in bafflement and hauled out his pipe.

Becker frowned as he increased his speed to pass a lumbering motor home with a Kansas license plate.

"We should do a time line on all of this. If the times are just right, it might be possible. I'd also like to know when the fair is busiest—when they take in the most money. That might give us a clue as to when a robbery would be most lucrative. With everything else going on, we haven't really had a chance to look into that. The management and security at the fair will have to be warned to take precautions."

"We'll do that as soon as we get back to town. But that warning, unfortunately, could make it harder, or impossible, to figure out who's responsible. For the moment, we've got to focus on what Ehlers has found for us—see about locating Jessie. I wonder if Jessie's hurt herself with that bad knee and is somewhere unable to get back to her truck. But if Wease didn't make that threatening phone call—and now we may never know—we've got to consider that someone out here may be involved in the robbery plot—that she got too close and was grabbed to keep her quiet. If Wease killed Belmont, that's one thing. Someone else killing Wease makes me very uneasy about her being missing."

As they sped past Nancy Lake, Becker glanced across and recognized the apprehension on his partner's face. Though he said nothing, he found it familiar because it matched his own.

On the road he had described to Becker on the phone, Lynn Ehlers and another man were waiting in a truck. A box used for transporting dogs took up the bed of it, covering the rear cab window and obscuring the rearview mirror, but in the side mirror he saw the two troopers pull up behind the vehicle. He immediately climbed out and came walking toward them.

"Hey, Phil," he said, offering a hand to Becker and a nod to Jensen, who had stood on the passenger side of the pickup after getting out. "Jensen."

"Dick Ray," he introduced his friend. "We work dogs together out of Dick's kennel."

"Where's this water jug?" Becker asked. "You move it?"

"No. I thought we'd better leave it where we found it for you to see. I don't like this one bit, Phil. It's out of place here."

As Ehlers led them around his truck, they could see that the road ended approximately fifty feet beyond the vehicle. A narrow trail extended beyond it, disappearing into a forest of spruce, birch, and shrubbery that was similar to but thicker than that which surrounded Jessie's cabin back on Knik Road.

"Over here."

Twenty feet in front of his truck, he stopped and pointed away from the road. Until they caught up to where he stood, the blue plastic water container that lay just a few feet from the uneven roadway was invisible in the brush.

Becker and Jensen both walked into the bushes to take a close look.

The container lay where it had fallen and was partially obscured by foliage. Pulling a bandana from his pocket, Jensen rolled it over and found "Arnold" printed on the other side, as they had been told.

"It's Jessie's, all right," he said. "I should know. I labeled this one a few weeks before the Yukon Quest." Picking it up by the handle with the bandana, he carried it carefully back to the road.

"There won't be prints unless someone tossed it back there," Becker said.

"There's some of mine on the neck of it," Ehlers informed them, noting the glance Jensen gave him.

"You never know. We'll send it in to John and see." Setting it down on the gravel, Jensen hunkered down to examine it scrupulously. All he could ascertain was that one side had a crack, indicating that it had landed hard.

Becker turned to Ehlers. "You look around?"

"Not after you said to stay put. The trail back there seems to have been used by a four-wheeler, but I have no idea where or how far it goes."

"Let's find out."

"Before we do that, you should see these." Closer to the disappearing trail, Ehlers showed them a set of tire tracks in the damp ground at the edge of the road. "I'm no expert, but these look like the same tread that I saw where Jessie's truck was found parked. I think her truck could have made these, too."

"You think she drove in here?"

"If she did, it looks like she parked there, then turned around and drove out again. It's a rough road, as you found out. That blue plastic thing could easily have bounced out without her noticing."

"Makes sense, but it's a good way from where her truck was found," Jensen commented, having secured the water container inside Becker's truck. "Why would she drive in here?"

"Just to turn around, maybe," Becker suggested.

"She could have done that closer to the highway, and there are no kennels on this road. Jessie knows them all. She would have known that. She wouldn't have parked if she were just turning around. Besides, it's an assumption that Jessie was behind the wheel. It could have been someone else."

The four stood looking down at the tire tracks on the ground. They were familiar to Jensen, who had seen similar tracks in Jessie's home driveway many times in the past.

"No one up this far saw her," Ehlers told him, "and they all know Jessie. We found the last people who remember seeing her—Judy Clark and Mose Atkinson. But that's back toward Nancy Lake on the other side of the highway from where her truck was found. She stopped to talk to them the morning she disappeared. I spoke to Ben Smith, who lives beyond them. He didn't see or talk to her, but he wasn't there that morning. He did see an unfamiliar truck headed out, as he came home later. The other kennel owner on that road wasn't home—if you call it a kennel. I wouldn't."

He curled a lip in disgust, turned and spat onto the road as if something vile had left its taste in his mouth.

"That bad?"

"Worse," Ehlers's friend Dick Ray spoke up for the first time. "We're going to report it. There's fifteen or twenty dogs back there, malnourished and going without water." He shook his head at the behavior of some people and angrily kicked a rock off the road. It ricocheted off a birch trunk and vanished into the brush.

"Who's the owner?" Becker asked.

But Jensen had swung around and was walking away toward the trail at the end of the road.

"Let's see where this leads us," he called back. "I don't believe Jessie would've come this far in just to turn around and drive back out. The truck was parked, and I want to know why."

With room for only one at a time on the narrow trail, they started along it single file, Jensen leading. Becker walked behind him, with Ehlers and Ray following closely.

The foliage at the top of the tall birches closed in overhead, blocking most of the light. The track was rough, with exposed roots in some places and depressions in others that slowed their pace. But there were sections that clearly showed tire tracks and recent wear from a four-wheeler. In places it was scarcely wide enough to allow even such a small vehicle to pass, but whoever used it had cut a tree now and then and evidently hacked at the brush with a machete. The signs of wheeled passage continued.

They had walked approximately a quarter of a mile when Jensen stopped and stepped away from the track. Reaching into the brush, he picked up a length of what looked to

Becker like rope. But when Jensen turned and held it out for the three behind him to see, it was a leash—the kind used to tether a dog.

"Shit," Becker said.

Without a word, Jensen folded the leash in half and in half again to make it easier to carry. He started on, moving even faster than before.

"I know this place," Dick Ray said suddenly. "I ran dogs on this trail last winter. There's an old prospector's cabin not too far from here. Beyond that, this trail hooks up to another that leads back to Nancy Lake."

"How far?" Jensen demanded over his shoulder, without slowing.

"Maybe as far as we've come from the road."

They went on, trotting now to keep up with the tall trooper who was stretching his long legs to cover ground rapidly without breaking into a run.

Briefly Becker pictured the abandoned body of Ron Wease, as they had found him on the floor of his bloody kitchen, and hoped. He did not allow himself to examine the suggestion of dread that hovered close behind that hope—just clung to the shred or two of optimism he could dredge up as he hurried after his friend and partner.

In total, they covered close to half a mile of winding trail before they found the old cabin Ray had mentioned. Trees had grown up around it over the years of its existence and abandonment, darkening the small clearing where the four men paused to assess the ancient building. Constructed of weathered logs, with a sagging sod roof, it appeared close to collapse—a natural return to the fallen and decaying logs that littered the floor of the forest and nurtured its growth.

Again Jensen led the way across the clearing to the wooden door of the cabin. It looked solid, obviously opened out, and was tightly closed. With a quick, unreadable glance at Becker, he stepped up and, taking firm hold of the rusty piece of iron that had been nailed on as a handle, gave it a yank. With a warning screech, the whole door came away from the frame, the nails that had held the hinges rusted through.

"Jeeze." Throwing up his arms, Jensen arrested its fall. The hand-hewn planks from which it was made were dry and weighed so little that he was easily able to lift it away from the opening and lean it against the log wall to one side. Without hesitation, he stepped through the doorway into the cabin, followed by the other three.

It was empty.

"Careful," he warned, waving a hand at the floor, which Becker could see was rotted through in more than one place, where the collapsing sod roof had allowed rain and snow to soak the planks of which it was made. Even the narrow beams that had supported the roof were bowed and broken. One had already fallen, scattering sod in lumps of dirt and dried grass beneath the resulting hole. In one corner, under another hole, a small, square cast-iron stove had dripped enough rust to dye the planks on which it rested.

"Look," Becker said, pointing.

They were hard to see in the dusk of the cabin's interior, but on one still solid part of the floor a double line of boot prints had disturbed the dust and dirt that lay upon it—going across to a small window and returning. Someone had walked across this dilapidated room—recently.

CHAPTER 23

Jensen said nothing until they had returned to the trucks they had parked on the side road. He had lifted and leaned the door back in its place and left the clearing last, allowing Becker to take the lead on the way out. Falling in behind Ehlers, he walked head down, silent and thoughtful.

"What now?" asked Ehlers when they stood by his pickup. "Somebody had obviously been there."

Jensen gave him a long look, then shrugged.

"Keep looking, I guess. There's got to be a reason that water container from Jessie's truck wound up beside this particular road. We'll send it to the lab, but I doubt we'll get much in the way of prints. Maybe she did just turn around and bounce it out. I wonder, though, why she didn't come to you for help when she headed out here yesterday morning. She would have had to pass your kennel, wouldn't she?"

"Yes. I've wondered that myself. Maybe she wanted to search by herself for some reason. She's like that sometimes."

There was a moment of silence while they stared at each other.

"Maybe she did," Jensen agreed finally, refusing to be drawn in by Ehlers's knowledgeable observation about Jessie.

Becker decided to break the tension. "Well, we've got to get back to town. There're two murder cases on our plate at the moment. You going to keep on here?"

"Yes—as long as it's light, or until we find Jessie."

When they were back in the truck and Becker was about to back out to give Ehlers room to reach the highway, Jensen held up a restraining hand. "Wait," he said. "Let them go first."

Becker complied, although this made it more difficult for Ehlers to turn his pickup around and meant he had to back it several times until he had clearance.

"What was that about?" Becker asked as the other truck swung onto the highway and disappeared, leaving a thin cloud of dust hanging in the air above the unpaved side road.

"You took a pretty good look at the boot prints in that cabin?"

"Yeah."

"How about the pattern of Ehlers's boots in the trail?"

"Didn't pay attention. Why?"

"Come and look," Jensen said, opening the cab door to climb out again.

They walked back to where the narrow trail began, and he pointed to a section of damp earth that was bare of fallen leaves and other forest detritus.

"He was walking right in front of me. I stepped around these last few prints he left—there."

Now familiar with the pattern of the prints he had crouched to examine in the cabin, Becker saw what Jensen meant.

"They look similar."

"More like the same. Redwings. I have a pair myself, on their way up here from Idaho in a box I had my mother mail."

"I couldn't swear to it without lab work—casts and photos. But if they're the same size and the minute details match . . ." Becker allowed his words to trail off in thought. "But why would Ehlers make tracks in that cabin, then take us there to see them?"

"I don't know, but I don't like it." Jensen's forehead creased in a frown.

"You want to get the boys from the lab out here to make sure of this?"

"It's not much to go on. Maybe later. Right now I want to know just who this Lynn Ehlers is—everything I can find out. I met him when Jessie ran the Quest, but I don't know anything about him really. It's time we did."

Becker got slowly to his feet and gave his partner an uneasy look.

"What?" Jensen asked.

"Alex, are you sure you aren't reacting to—"

"To whatever—ah—*friendship* he has with Jessie? Am I just jealous—out to get him?"

"Could have sliced the tension in pieces back there. Might as well get it out and take a look at it."

Jensen turned without answering and walked away toward the truck, where he climbed into the passenger seat and waited for Becker.

They had driven several miles toward Palmer in silence when he finally responded.

"Maybe you're right, Phil. I think I'm aware enough of the strain between us to set it aside, but—maybe not. Still those prints are so much the same it worries me. I didn't make them up. There are a few other things. *He* volunteered to look for Jessie. *He* found the water container and made a point of explaining any prints of his that are found on it. Pretty convenient, isn't it? I'd be suspicious of anyone else under the same circumstances. I can't treat Ehlers any different, can I?"

"From that angle, it makes sense to take a look," Becker admitted. "But other parts of it don't make sense, Alex. What connection does Ehlers have with Wease and Belmont? If Wease was Jessie's caller and in on a robbery plan, where does Ehlers fit in?"

"It's a small town. They could have met since he moved up here from Minnesota. Look, all I really want is to find Jessie. Her being missing for a few hours would tell me there might be something wrong. This amount of time elapsed makes me sure there is. Where the hell is she, dammit?"

Becker drove on, thinking hard about the division of Jensen's attention. Jensen's worry about Jessie was growing by the hour, while at the same time he was trying to concentrate on the rest of the confusion that confronted them both.

"Look," Becker suggested abruptly, "I think we should split up. You concentrate on finding Jessie. I'll concentrate on these murders and the connections. I can talk to the boy and the old man. We can cover more ground and maybe come up with some answers."

For a long moment Jensen was silent. Then he nodded agreement. "Okay. Let's do it."

Danny's parents retrieved their son at the senior center and brought Frank Monroe along with him to meet the troopers at Becker's office. There Becker heard from both about Danny's flight from the man in the truck and his panicked arrival at the senior center. Danny had not stopped to take a good look at his pursuer, so his description was lacking in details, but he was sure he could recognize the man again if he saw him.

"You hadn't seen the man before, but you would know him if you saw him again, right?"

"Yeah, sure I would! He got out of his truck and tried to grab me." Danny's face twisted with anxiety as he remembered.

"I might want you to look at some people to see if you could pick him out," Becker said.

From Danny's expression, he was not happy at the idea. But when Frank Monroe laid a hand on his shoulder and assured him that he would have protection and company, he nodded and agreed.

"There has to be a reason why he came after you," Becker told them. "Can either one of you think of a reason?"

They both shook their heads.

"What kind of truck was it?" he asked.

"Brown and white," Monroe answered. "Might have been a Chevy. But it came and went so rapidly that I had no opportunity to examine the license plate. I did observe that it was Alaskan, however."

Becker decided to let it go for the moment and asked for details of their two days at the fairground.

The boy was much more willing to talk about his adventures in escaping Ron Wease and hiding out. He talked for five minutes, telling it all, with Monroe adding a word or two of clarification.

"Parts of it were scary, but it was fun, most of the time," Danny finished.

"What did you like best?" Becker asked.

"Doing things with Mr. Monroe—like being a scarecrow and sleeping under the table. And I really liked the dog."

"What dog?"

"There was a woman named Jessie at the booth for the Iditarod. She let me pet her dog named Tank. She said you had to be really responsible if you had a dog. I'm going to try to be really responsible." He cast a quick look at his father to see if this statement had registered.

"I'm glad to hear it," Doug Tabor told him, knowing exactly where his son's promise was aimed, and suppressing a grin.

"Did you see the dog or Jessie again after that?" Becker asked hopefully.

"Nope. I was going to, but I got chased after that, so I didn't go back."

"Did you see the man who chased you with anyone else at the fairground?"

The boy frowned, trying to remember. "Yes," he said finally. "When I was hiding under the cabin he talked to a man with rainbow hair, and they walked off together."

"Rainbow hair?"

"You know—they dye it at the fair—all different colors. It went out in points." He made pulling motions with both hands from his scalp into the air to illustrate what he meant.

"I remember that vendor," Monroe smiled. "The spikes of hair made him somewhat resemble the Statue of Liberty, but each one was a different color. We observed the man who chased you with someone else, too, Danny. He was with another security guard in front of the office when we intended to turn in the bag the first time, remember? You hid in the T-shirt rack."

They related that incident, then told about hearing Wease in conversation with the barn manager and on the phone on their first night under the table. When they were finished, Becker, who had been making notes, asked Danny about another time and place.

"Tell me more about the two men you saw arguing behind The Sluice Box," he requested. "What did they look like?"

"It was too dark to see much, but one had a blue jacket. The other one—the one who chased me when I *accidentally* took the red bag? He was taller."

Becker had hoped the boy would at least be able to put Wease and Belmont together. Ready to go on to another question, he swallowed it, gratification flooding in as Danny continued.

"But I saw the one with the blue jacket before. He got

pushed out the back door of The Sluice Box, and then I saw his face."

"Before you saw them arguing?"

"Yeah."

"Who pushed him?"

"I didn't know him. Some big guy."

"Is this the man who got pushed?" He handed Danny a mug shot of Belmont obtained from police records.

Danny's eyes widened as he stared at the picture and nodded.

"His hair was shorter than this."

"Did you see him anywhere else?"

"No. It was the other one that chased me."

Becker set another empty bottle of Killian's on the hearth by Jessie's stove.

"I asked them everything I could think of that might help," he said, turning to the boy. "You were very good at remembering things, Danny. Danny?"

But Danny had drifted off with one arm around the dog. Curled up on the rug at Jessie's feet he and Tank were both sound asleep.

His mother shifted in her seat. "Oh dear. We'd better take him home, Doug."

"He's fine." Jessie grinned. "They both are. Be kind of a shame to separate such good buddies."

Jill settled back, amused at the picture made by the sleeping pair.

"Okay, if you're sure. I would like to know how the rest of this

happened. You know, Doug, I think we might consider getting Danny a dog sometime soon."

Her husband rolled his eyes.

"He's still grounded and has to finish his chores before we talk about that," he said, but didn't dismiss the idea completely.

"So it was Belmont who Eric threw out of The Sluice Box while Hank and I were there," Jessie said, remembering.

"Yes," Becker agreed. "Eric was also one of the people on our list. We knew he and Belmont had had an altercation earlier, that Eric had barred him from the pub, and told him not to come back. Their confrontation supposedly got pretty heated, so we checked him out."

"Eric's an okay guy, but I can understand your thinking. You checked out one of the lumberjacks, too, didn't you?"

"There was one who substituted once in a while who had no alibi. We had him on our list for a while, but eventually he was cleared by one of the other guys in the show."

"And you were out on the road searching for me," Jessie said to Jensen. "I wish I'd known that anyone was looking for me. It would have made things easier—for me and maybe for Tank."

CHAPTER 24

We drove back to town, where I picked up Jessie's truck, a radio, some bottled water and supplies. I even tossed in a sleeping bag. At that point I was stubborn—determined to stay till I found her or something that would lead to her, and I didn't know how long that would take. I went out the road and started looking. I didn't trust anything I hadn't seen or heard for myself, so I retraced a lot of ground and talked to a lot of people who told me things I already knew.

"Some time after four o'clock that afternoon, Ehlers and Ray passed me on the highway headed back to feed their dogs and themselves before they started looking again. We divided up the areas that hadn't been searched. I took the side roads beyond where we'd found the water jug. They said they'd search the ones on the other side of the highway."

"That's a lot of territory," Timmons commented.

"Yeah, it was." Jensen turned to Jessie. "And I kept remembering the feeling I had when we reached that old prospector's cabin, before I got the door open. We already had two people dead and—"

"And you thought you might find me dead, too." Jessie made it easier by interrupting to state the obvious herself.

"It crossed my mind."

"Hell," Becker said, "it crossed all our minds. It was so totally unacceptable that we refused to entertain it out loud, but we had all admitted to ourselves that it was possible."

"Yes," Jessie said softly, thinking back. "I had begun to think it was more than possible. I had no idea where I was, so how could anyone else? With another night on the way, I was terrified for Tank. I didn't know how much longer he could be expected to obey me. There had to be a limit. I knew I could hold out a lot longer than he could, or would, but he would stay on that platform longer if I was awake to keep telling him. I was so tired and my muscles were cramped in knots. It hurt like bones were being broken. But if I relaxed, even for a minute, if I went to sleep . . ." She hesitated and let the sentence trail away, then sat up straighter, another emotional memory surfacing.

"I was so angry*! I'm still angry. I'd had a long time to think and I knew that whoever had put us there meant for me to be* that *terrified and* that *angry. Damn him! He* wanted *me to watch Tank die*—meant *it to happen. Why? I'll never understand how anyone can hate that much.*

"I didn't know if he would come back to gloat, but I thought he might. I think he wanted me to wonder if he'd come and kill me, too. So I was torn between the impossible choices that he'd left

me. Knowing that I couldn't escape without sacrificing Tank—I'd already tried the only thing I could think of and it didn't work—actually made things worse. If Tank were dead I might be able to pull the board over the beams with the chain. Then there would be a chance of getting out of there before the bastard came back—if he was coming back. Or I could stay and hope he'd let us both go. But what if he didn't come back at all? Worst of all, I knew that Tank might die no matter what I did. The lowest point was when I realized that part of me wished it was over—almost wished Tank would try to get down and settle it."

Jessie lapsed into guilty silence at this admission, as startled at the intensity of her outburst as were those gathered in the room. Though Danny slept on, Tank had heard his name and raised his head to watch her closely. He whined, sensitive to her distress, and she laid a trembling hand on his head.

"Jessie?" Frank Monroe said quietly after a minute.

She looked up at him, eyes wide, half her mind still out there somewhere in the dark.

"It's all right, Jessie. Tank is all right and so are you. Come back here where it's warm and bright. We love you."

As the afternoon progressed and the sun fell low enough to cast long arms of shadow across the highway, Jensen, driving through the alternating bars of light and shade, almost missed a slim side road that went into the forest at an angle. Continuing past it, he turned around at the next driveway, went back, and turned onto this suggestion of a road.

It was narrower than those he had already searched, and pitted with deep potholes that had never been graded smooth or graveled. But it exhibited some use in a number of tracks that had been made by tires when the ground was wet and then dried into ruts in the mud. Dust swirled up behind Jessie's truck as he followed the road, which rocked and bounced the vehicle, jarring him roughly. A bottle of water rolled off the seat on the passenger's seat to dance a jig of rebounds on the floor.

The road grew so narrow it became a track. Sharp talons of heavy brush clawed at the paint on both sides of the truck, screeching like fingernails on a blackboard. Jensen wrestled the vehicle around two sharp bends that had been created to avoid the effort of cutting trees and quite suddenly came to its end, on the banks of a creek, where he could drive no farther. For a long minute or two he sat in the cab, engine running, grateful to have the world grow still, and considered that he would have to back the truck over the whole quarter mile he had just traveled when he was ready to leave.

It was dark under the canopy of the birch, and the thick black spruce seemed to absorb light. The dust his passing had created caught up and rolled past the truck, encouraged by a slight breeze. For a minute or two it obscured his view of the creek and its banks, and a little of it settled on the sleeve of the elbow he had rested on the open window frame. Then, as the air cleared, he noticed something oddly bulky beside a tree on the far side, where a trail of sorts seemed to continue into the forest.

Silencing the engine, he climbed from the cab and reached back for his windbreaker, which he put on. Retrieving the water bottle from the floor, he twisted off the cap and drank, then stuffed it in the pocket of his jacket before he shut and locked the door.

At the dull sound of the door closing, a startled squirrel dashed across the track in front of the truck and up a tree, where it sat sending out a *tic-tic-tic* of warning. Jensen could hear its small claws scrabble on the spruce bark as it climbed to a higher branch and recommenced its alarm. *Tic-tic-tic.* He listened for a moment and looked toward the source of the sounds until he located the bright eyes that glared resentfully down at the intruder.

Turning, he walked quickly to the creek and looked across at the bulky object he had noticed from inside the truck. It was still unidentifiable; so he considered just how to avoid the most mud and water in gaining the opposite bank to take a closer look. At this point the creek had widened into a marshy area about fifteen feet across, which judging from several defining ruts was the result of a wheeled vehicle breaking down the banks in going back and forth through the water. To the left, where the banks were unbroken, three birch trunks had been cut and dropped over the flow. Dark bits of mud and a leaf or two clung to these from the feet of someone who had used them as a bridge. Jensen did the same, sustaining his balance with spread arms as the slender trunks gave under his weight.

Once across, he stepped to the object under investigation and found that it was covered by a plastic tarp printed in camouflage and fastened with bungee cords to keep the curious wind from twitching it loose. Unfastening the cords, he stripped back the tarp and tossed it aside to reveal a four-wheel vehicle with space for a single seated rider, possibly two. A rack in the rear allowed for carrying a limited amount of cargo. Many people in the area used similar rigs on expeditions into the wilderness during hunting season. Others used them to reach weekend cabins that were purposely built away from any road, and to carry supplies to them.

The engine was cold, had not been used recently enough to retain heat. He reached for the tarp. If the outside of it was covered with grime, there was no telling how long it had rested there unmoved. But it was relatively clean, indicating that it had not been long since it was used to cover the four-wheeler.

The bushes on which the tarp had landed swayed as he pulled it toward him, and something bright fell out of them to the ground at his feet. Bending, he picked up an orange bandana folded diagonally, with the two extended corners tied together.

Jensen stared at the object in his hand, his mind racing. He recognized, not this particular bit of fabric, but the form of it—the way it was knotted. Jessie sometimes tied similar ones around her dogs' necks—especially Tank's—loose, so if it caught on something it would slip over the dog's head easily to avoid strangling. This bandana was new, crisp and clean, had never been laundered. Raising it to his nose, Jensen sniffed at it. It smelled of dog.

In half a dozen strides he was back across the birch-trunk bridge on his way to the truck. Juicing up the radio, he tried to call the dispatcher and got back nothing but static. Too far away, too much in between. Slipping the bandana on his arm and sliding it up his jacket sleeve where he could see it, he slung the backpack he had prepared over one shoulder, once again locked the cab, and headed off into the forest. He hesitated before passing the four-wheeler and thought about using it, but not knowing what, or who, he might find, decided to do without the noise it would create.

The track was much less of a trail than the one he and Becker had followed with Ehlers and Ray earlier in the day. A snake would have crawled straighter. It wound on and on, barely wide enough to allow access for the four-wheeler he had elected not to use, though in several places he saw tire prints that were fresh since the last rain and boot prints that matched those he had seen on the other trail as well. They brought Ehlers back to mind. The forest grew darker as the day slowly faded behind him, but it was just light enough to make his way. For close to half an hour he walked.

While he was still in the thick of the trail, Jensen's ears suddenly told him there was something foreign as the muffled sound of a human voice floated into them from—somewhere. He stopped, uncertain, trying to decide if he had actually heard anything at all and, if he had, which direction it had come from. The silence was extreme. Not a squirrel or a bird song broke it. Could it have been the babble of the creek he heard? Perhaps its path twisted through the woods and he was coming close to it again. As he stood like one of the motionless trees, a low crooning sound came again, continued, hesitated; then, as he strained to hear, the breeze picked up and blew it away in the rustle of leaves. He waited, but it did not repeat itself. Not running water, then.

He stepped forward on the trail, which looped left around a bushy spruce, then turned right through a patch of tall brush. It grew a little lighter ahead. The trail straightened for a few feet, and he hurried along it almost at a trot.

There was a suggestion of that sound again, definitely off to the right this time, and he realized he was passing the source of it. Retracing his steps, he saw that in the tall brush he had missed the hint of a division in the trail. A branch ran away between a large pair of spruce with branches that reached almost across it.

Pushing his way through, he stepped out into an area without the birch trees to shut out the light with their dense leaf canopy. Only young spruce grew quite thick in the space. Like guardians they surrounded another old cabin so densely that all he could see was one corner, where the logs from which it was built dovetailed together in a typical alternating pattern. Cautious now, he walked around it until he found himself facing a door similar to the one he had yanked from its frame on the other cabin.

It was tightly closed.

There was no sound at all from within.

CHAPTER 25

The fair was still crowded with people that evening when Phil Becker drove onto the grounds and parked his truck in the employee lot behind The Sluice Box. Instead of going directly to the pub, where he had arranged to meet the head of security, Dave Lomax, he took a rear entrance into the arena where the lumberjack shows were over for the day and walked slowly across to the pond where Belmont's body had been discovered.

The bleachers on the western side of the arena were high enough to obstruct the last light of the sinking sun and cast the central space into deep shadow. To the south, the peaks of the Chugach Mountains were so pink with alpine glow that they could have been rose quartz. The surface of the logrolling pond rippled slightly in the breeze and became a kaleidoscope of glowing gold, purple, and red reflected from the sunset, but the water beneath was so dark it seemed deeper than it actually was.

For a few minutes Becker stood looking down into it thoughtfully. Then he turned away and strolled slowly around the perimeter of the arena.

Chunks of logs were stacked to one side of the bleachers waiting to be used the next day by the lumberjacks in demonstrations of skills with ax and saw. Two tall tree trunks, denuded of limbs and bark, had been raised beyond the pond for climbing races. Next to them, wheels sliced from the large end of a log had been mounted on posts and painted in black, yellow, and red concentric circles—targets for competitions in throwing axes like the one that had killed Belmont.

Becker stood staring at these. He often played games of darts with friends, but found it amazing that anyone could hurl a heavy ax end over end through the air to hit anything.

"Broad side of a barn, maybe," he muttered to himself at the idea of trying it. The yard-wide targets seemed very small for such an activity, and he decided that it must take a lot of practice.

The ax they had found in the dead man's skull had not been hurled, but swung in an arc over the perpetrator's head. Considering that, even from the downward angle at which it had penetrated, it was impossible to accurately judge the killer's height. From the weight of the ax, the killer had to have been significantly strong to be able to swing it, and experience with the tool seemed necessary to hit such a minimal target. Belmont's head, Becker remembered, had been just about the size of the red innermost circle on the targets—approximately eight inches, ear to ear.

Shaking his head at the thought, he turned away and left the arena through the arch that led to the area behind The Sluice Box, wondering if perhaps he should take another look at the lumberjacks instead of assuming that Wease was responsible.

But you know," he said, thinking back to that evening and his speculations, "most of the people in the bush all over the state use those axes all the time, and some of them are better than any lumberjack with them. The killer could have been any one of them. There were things we just didn't know yet. Wease seemed most likely, but we couldn't prove it. Then there was the additional problem of who had killed him and left him to bleed out on his kitchen floor. I figured that the butcher knife that sliced his throat was another weapon of opportunity—that both murders might have happened pretty much on the spur of the moment, with no prior intent. So I set out to see what else I could learn—and to warn the security people at the fair about the robbery we thought was being planned."

The Sluice Box was close to half full, though the crowd was steadily growing in anticipation of the live musical entertainment that would begin in less than an hour—a bluegrass ensemble this time. People seeking good seats had already filled the picnic tables nearest the stage, and a few stood at the tall tables near the front door.

Dave Lomax, something of a ladies' man, was leaning against the bar in conversation with a good-looking blond woman who was casually responding to his flirting while keeping her hands busy filling plastic cups with beer from the taps. Catching sight of Becker, he raised a hand in the trooper's direction, glanced at his watch, and asked the woman a question. She shrugged and gave him a noncommittal smile, but rolled her eyes and winked at Becker as Lomax turned away.

While he was making his farewells, Eric, the bartender, came out from the cooler behind the bar, frowned slightly at the sight of Lomax, then noticed Becker waiting by the door. Nodding in recognition, he came across the room and put out a hand that was damp and cold from manhandling heavy metal beer kegs in the back room.

"Eric Glenn," he said, reintroducing himself to Becker.

"I remember."

"We heard Jessie Arnold had gone missing. Has she been found yet?"

"Not yet, but there's a lot of people looking for her."

"Damn. She's a friend. If I wasn't working, I'd go help."

"You may be able to help about another thing," Becker told him. "Did you throw a guy out of here through the back door night before last?"

Eric pursed his lips, trying to remember. In the busy pub, hours, days, and people tended to blur together.

"Yeah," he said, the incident springing to mind. "I did. There's always a couple of good-time Charlies to create a problem during the fair. I eighty-sixed him earlier that night, but he came back and tried to shove into the beer line. The front door was crowded, so I tossed him out the back. Oh—and that was the night Jessie was here. It was a hoot. Hobo Jim did his wolf howl song and her dog joined right in."

"Is this the guy you tossed?"

Becker offered the picture of Belmont.

"Sure is. He in trouble?"

"Not now. He's the dead guy we pulled out of the pond."

"No shit?"

"You know anything else about him? Ever see him with anyone?"

"Saw him with Ron Wease a couple of times. Not that night, though."

"Wease in here at all that night?"

"Not that I remember."

"Okay, thanks, Eric. If you think of anything . . ."

"I'll let you know."

Dave Lomax walked up to join them and immediately Eric turned to go back to his job behind the bar.

"Let me hear what you find out about Jessie," he called back over his shoulder.

"Soon as we know something," Becker promised and watched him get back to work pouring beer for thirsty customers.

The crowd in the pub had increased significantly. "Let's get out of here," he suggested to Lomax. "Go somewhere we can hear ourselves talk."

As they left through the front door, Lomax paused to check with the pub's assigned security guard.

"Everything okay here, Ted?"

"Fine. Pretty mellow so far."

They strolled toward the plaza at the center of the fairground, Becker enjoying the atmosphere of people having a good time. There were still lines at most of the food vendors' booths, an especially long one for barbecued ribs—partly the result of the tempting smell of grilled meat that wafted through the air to draw in customers. Roasted turkey legs were another popular item.

In the blue half-dark that comes just after the sun has set, the fair's multitude of colored lights took on a glow that seemed brighter than at any other time. He glanced back to see the Ferris wheel spinning high over the midway in a jeweled circle that was almost magical against the darkening sky. He wished he could be on it looking down.

"So," Lomax inquired at his side, "what's up?"

Reluctantly Becker set aside his momentary appreciation and brought his mind to bear on the problem at hand.

"You talking to him about that guy who got killed and dumped in the pond?" Lomax asked.

"Curtis Belmont. The night he was killed he caused a problem in The Sluice Box and got tossed out. You know him?"

"Just who he is. But I've seen him around—with Ron Wease a time or two."

So witnesses had now solidly linked Wease and Belmont. Becker filed the confirmation away and changed the subject.

"Look," he said, "we think there may be a potential robbery in the works—aimed at one day of the fair receipts."

"Robbery? You gotta be kidding. What we take in goes out heavily guarded. Only a few people even know where it's brought from the gates and accumulated. Belmont involved?"

"Some reason you think he might have been?"

"You were talking about him."

"It's possible, but we don't know. He and Wease may both have been involved, but there have to be others we haven't identified yet. There's some evidence that points to robbery as a possibility."

"What evidence?" the security director demanded.

"Pictures taken in the morning before the fair opened. They show an armored truck coming and going from the place you keep the money overnight. That red building—right there."

They had reached the plaza, and Becker pointed across the wide space at the innocuous building that looked like nothing but a food vendor's booth. "That is the right one, isn't it?"

Lomax's mouth dropped open. "How the hell?"

"Take a look." Becker handed him one of the photos showing the parked truck and two uniformed men carrying bags of money from the building's back door to load into the vehicle.

In the light from a cappuccino wagon, Lomax stared at it for a long moment without speaking. Then he began to swear. Softly, but vehemently, he used what must have been close to his entire repertoire of curses before handing the picture back.

"Where did you get this?"

"From Wease's bag that kid accidentally took. Because Wease wanted it back so badly, we were suspicious and had several rolls of his exposed film developed. We looked these over late yesterday."

"What now?"

"Now," said Becker, "I think we'd better get together with whoever else on the management staff needs to be told and figure out how to handle this. What I need is to know who else is in on this thing. Someone who wasn't Wease—or, obviously, Belmont, since he was already dead—chased the boy again this morning. He saw the man—can identify him. I'd like to bring him over to see if he can pick anyone out of your security staff."

"Why my staff?"

"Because Wease was working for you, and it makes good sense. We've got to start somewhere."

"Well, Wease won't be a problem anymore, will he?"

"Why not?" Becker asked, startled, wondering how Lomax could possibly know about Wease's murder so soon, when he and Jensen had decided to keep the information to themselves for the time being.

"Well, because—I already told you—I fired him, didn't I?"

It was true, Becker remembered. He had.

CHAPTER 26

Jensen stared blankly at the wooden door of the cabin he had found, apprehensive about opening it for a second or two, unsure of what might be inside. Listening intently, he heard nothing but the sigh of the breeze as it rustled birch leaves at the edges of the clearing and the harsh complaint of a raven from somewhere in the surrounding forest.

Instead of a wooden or metal handle, this door had a cast iron latch with a curved bar that lifted to disengage the simple mechanism that held it closed. Hoping the hinges on this door would not give way, Jensen took firm hold of the latch bar with the fingers of one hand and lifted it. The door swung inward as he leaned against it, but the iron hinges shrieked in resistance. There were immediate scrambling sounds inside, and a dog barked once.

"No. Stay," a voice he almost didn't recognize commanded desperately.

Jensen stepped through the door into the cabin, but it was so dark that at first he could see nothing but a pale square of dying daylight that fell through a small window on one wall, empty except for a shard or two of broken glass.

"No-o-o," the ragged voice howled from the far side of the room. Something hit the floor with a thump, and from eye level and to the left a black shadow came hurtling out of the dark directly at Jensen.

Throwing up his arms in defense, he was startled when the attacking form seemed to stop abruptly in midair. It fell in an arc just short of him and swung back and forth, struggling and making constricted animal sounds, suspended a few feet from where he stood.

"No. Oh, please, *no*. Don't let him die." The plea in the voice was now wild with frustration and pain. "*Please*. Help him."

He could hear another struggle going on across the room. What sounded like a chain rattled on wood overhead, and he could just make out a human figure straining with both arms toward the ceiling against a restraint that held it there, trying at the same time to fling itself toward the dangling form.

"Jessie?"

The voice grew more frantic in its appeal. "Help him, dammit. *Do something*."

As Jensen's sight finally adjusted to what dim light the window afforded, he realized with horror that the struggling form that hung struggling by its neck from an overhead beam was a dog. *Tank*.

"Oh God—oh God. Please—no," Jessie wailed.

Stepping swiftly forward, he caught up the animal with one arm and raised a hand to loosen the constricting cord around its neck. Barely conscious, the dog lay limp in his arms. He gave it a sharp hug and its body convulsed in a deep gasp. Still sucking air back into his lungs, Tank was otherwise quiet when Jensen laid him gently on the plank floor in front of him.

"It's okay," he told Jessie, relieved. "He'll be all right."

Still panting, Tank raised his head toward the familiar voice of the man he idolized, had recognized, and had attempted to reach with one joyous but deadly leap.

Jensen laid a hand on the dog's head to reassure him, but his concern now was all for the woman across the room. He could hear her weeping where she hung by the arms from a chain that held her in a reaching position under another beam.

In two huge strides, he was across the room and supporting her in the circle of one arm while he reached to release her, as he had Tank. But this time it was not so simple. A small but strong padlock held the tight links of chain around her wrists.

"Alex?" Jessie asked hoarsely, leaning back to see his face. "Where the hell did you come from?"

"Idaho," he answered, concentration elsewhere.

To his astonishment, she giggled through her tears.

"I can't get this off," he growled, annoyed.

"I know," she agreed quietly. "You'll have to let me go and get the chain loose from the board Tank was lying on. Then we can pull it across the beams and get it off me later."

"What board?"

She nodded across the room, where the rectangle of plywood had fallen when Tank made his affectionate leap.

As he assessed the situation and with her help figured out how the two had been confined, Jensen's wrath intensified.

"Who did this?" he demanded, furious and working hard with the back edge of the hunting knife he had carried on his belt to bend the nails and release the chain from the plywood.

"I don't know. He made sure I never saw his face."

The chain came loose. He tossed it over one beam, then pulled it over the other, allowing Jessie to lower her arms and collapse onto the floor with his assistance.

"Please—tell me you have water."

Jensen pulled the water bottle from his pocket and helped her to drink a few swallows.

She sighed with relief. "Tank, too."

The dog had regained his feet and come padding across the room to sit close beside his mistress. Lacking a container, Jensen poured water into the cup of one palm again and again, until the dog had had a good drink. Then he gave the rest to Jessie.

Though her wrists were still bound, with no tension to maintain on the chain her hands were painfully coming back to life. Ignoring that, she raised them over Tank's head and pulled him onto her lap, where she hugged and cuddled him like the puppy he had once been.

"You were such a good dog," she told him, rubbing her face against his cheek. "I love you, good boy. Oh, Alex, it's been such a long time, and I was so afraid he would jump down, or I'd let him fall off that thing."

One arm providing support around her, he felt her whole body begin to shake with residual anxiety and stress.

"You didn't," he reassured her. "You're both safe, and we can discuss it all later. Now we need to get out of here and get you taken care of."

"Yes—okay."

"There's food in your truck," Jensen told her.

"Good, we're starving. You found my *truck*?"

"Yes, but it's a long way, over a mile. Can you walk?"

"If you help me, I can hobble, but I've done something bad to this knee again trying to get us loose. I'll make it. I'm not staying here, for sure—wherever *here* is."

"You don't know?"

"Have no idea. I got hit and woke up here—like you found me."

They wound up the chain they couldn't remove from Jessie's wrists so it could be carried. Then, before they closed the cabin door behind them, Jensen cut down the length of yellow nylon cord that had strangled Tank and tucked it in his pocket.

It took a long time to go back along the ragged trail and was full dark by the time they reached the end of the track and could make out the truck parked on the other side of the creek.

Jensen glanced at the shape of the four-wheeler as they passed it. "He must have used that to take you in there."

Ignoring the bridge of birch trunks, Jensen scooped Jessie

up and carried her across the creek. Tank splashed through beside them.

They found a flashlight and a pair of bolt cutters in the supply of tools that Jessie always carried in a lockbox in the bed of her pickup, so Jensen was able to sever a link of the chain and free her arms. The beam of the light exposed extensive abrasions and deep purple bruises encircling her wrists, infuriating him all over again. But he bit his tongue and said nothing as he applied first aid from the kit that was also in the lockbox. For now anger could wait. Her injuries needed treatment, as did the more serious problem of her knee. But he was determined that whoever was responsible would not wait long.

There were other things—things between the two of them—that required attention. Those things would have to wait as well. For the time being he was satisfied to have found her, and Tank, alive and relatively unscathed.

"Where did you get that bandana?" Jessie asked, catching sight of the bright orange fabric that still hung around his jacket sleeve.

"It fell out of a bush on the other side of the creek," he told her. "Made me think Tank, at least, might be in there."

While he drove, Jessie ravenously ate bread and cheese washed down with water as if it were caviar and champagne, sharing equal amounts with Tank. An apple quickly followed, and half a bag of potato chips.

The food hit her empty stomach like a sleep-inducing drug. By the time they passed Houston on the way to Palmer, she was asleep, with Tank lying awake and on guard at her feet and her head against Jensen's shoulder. Before she faded completely, she laid one numb hand gently on his knee to attract his attention. He glanced over to see the reflection of the truck's headlights in her wide gray eyes and had a sudden memory of the first time he had met her, years before, in Rainy Pass during an Iditarod race. There had been a bonfire by a frozen lake, and he recalled seeing tiny reflections of its glow in her eyes then, too.

"Thank you," she said quietly.

"You're welcome," he returned, looking back to the road ahead.

She smiled, closed her eyes, and was gone.

I was so tired." Jessie smiled. "It was like falling into deep water. I don't remember a single thought crossing my mind before I crashed. I was just glad to be safe. It was as if somebody turned out the lights, then turned them back on again when we got to the hospital in Palmer."

"You barely woke up then," Jensen told her. "Do you remember being carried into emergency?"

"Vaguely. But I certainly woke right up when they started pouring disinfectant on my hands and arms."

She glanced down at her wrists, where a few scabs over healing abrasions and a fading yellowish bruise or two still showed.

"How's your knee, Jessie?" Timmons asked.

"Better, thanks."

CHAPTER 27

Paged from the fairground, where he had been meeting with management to decide how to guard against a robbery on very little information, Becker came into the Palmer hospital's emergency room at a jog to find Jensen sitting in the waiting area, elbows on knees, face cradled in the palms of his hands. Tank sat at his feet, alertly watching what went on around them.

"You found her! Where? How is she?"

Taking a chair next to the two, he reached to rub Tank's ears. "Tank okay?"

Jensen sat up and blinked for a minute without answering, pulling his thoughts back to focus on his partner's question. "They were both in a cabin about a mile farther up the road—similar to the one we found empty earlier."

"You let Ehlers know, so they can stop looking?"

Jensen shook his head, frowning. "Came straight in. She's pretty banged up, but nothing too serious. Tore up her knee again and has some bad scrapes and bruises from the chain the bastard used on her wrists."

"I'll call him. So she *was* snatched. Who was it?"

"She doesn't know—didn't get a look at him."

"Damn." Becker scowled in irritation. "What did she tell you?"

"Not much more than that, and it can wait till tomorrow. She's physically and mentally exhausted, Phil—hadn't eaten since she went missing until I fed her what I had in the truck. She slept all the way here. We'll have a few words when the doctor's through in there." He waved a hand at the hospital's interior. "He wants her overnight, and I want an officer outside her door."

"Fine," Becker agreed. "I'll take care of it. You going to stay here?"

"No. As soon as she's settled, I'm taking Tank back to her place. She wasn't happy not to have him with her, but they won't allow it. So she wants me to take him home, where I can keep him inside for the night and take him to the vet in the morning."

"What had this guy—whoever it was—done to her? You said *chained*?"

Jensen related all he could remember about what he had found, and as he talked, Becker could see how justifiably angry he was at the treatment Jessie had endured. Pounding one fist on his knee in bitter frustration, he ended the account, gave Becker a glance, and fell coldly silent for a moment.

"I'm going to get this guy, Phil—one way or another," he pledged.

"*We'll* get him."

I brought Tank back here," Jensen told the group in Jessie's living room. "He didn't want to leave you there, Jess. It was all I could do to get him in the truck. He trusts me, so he was okay once we got on the road, but once we got here, he wouldn't let me out of his sight. Every time I got up for anything, he got up, too. He ate a good dinner and drank water till I thought he'd float away. He was uneasy without you, so I slept on the sofa, so he could be there on the rug close to me."

They were back early the next morning to find Jessie better after a night of much-needed rest. She was dressed and sitting on her hospital bed, somewhat clumsily finishing what appeared to have been a huge breakfast.

"My hero," she greeted Jensen with a smile, laying down the soupspoon with which she had been shoveling scrambled eggs. "How's Tank?"

"Dropped him off at the vet. He's checking him out, but thinks he'll be fine."

"Good. Billy taking care of the rest of my mutts?"

"I called him last night, and he's been there every day, so they're fine, too. I called your friend Maxie. She's in Fort Nelson, headed for Alberta today. She's called every night worrying about you. Said to tell you to call her tonight if you can."

"I will. You'd like her. She's great."

She turned her attention to Becker as she attempted to push away the breakfast tray on its rolling support.

He took over and did it for her.

"Phil! I could have guessed you'd show up official-like." Then, in anticipation, "Don't say it. I know I shouldn't have gone off alone to look for him, but who knew?"

"Wasn't gonna," he told her with an I-give-up shrug of the shoulders and a grin that turned to grimace as he took in her swollen hands and the dressings on her wrists. "How're you doing?"

"Pretty good." She rubbed at her right hand with the fingers of the left. "Both hands are still half numb, but they say it'll go away when the swelling goes down. And there's good news. The doc that fixed my knee was in, took X rays, and says it won't need more surgery. I'm back to a brace for a while, and then we'll see, but it's probably just a setback. *And*—I can go home today—now, if you'll take me."

While she had been bringing them up-to-date on her medical condition, Becker had dragged up chairs for himself and Jensen. He took out a notebook and settled in one of them.

"Great! We'll see about that."

Jessie frowned. "What do you mean, *we'll see?* I want out of here and back in my own space."

Jensen, who had remained standing, strolled to the foot of the bed and gave her a serious look.

"There's a lot been going on while you weren't here, Jess," he told her. "Things you don't know that we think are involved with what happened to you. So if we're going to catch whoever did this to you—and Tank—we need to ask some questions. And you need to know some of what we've already learned."

"Like what?"

"Why don't we start with your telling us everything that happened to you—from the time you started out the Parks Highway to when Alex found you in that old cabin," Becker suggested. "It would help if we could get a look at it from your side first."

Jensen agreed and, as Jessie began her account of the last two days, finally sat down. They let her tell it all without interruption, though parts of what she related soon had Jensen pacing the floor again, glowering in self-controlled silence, suppressed anger making him restless.

"So," she finished by telling him, "you came and found us and brought us back here. That's it."

No one said anything for a minute, while Becker ran a pencil down the list of notes he had been taking during Jessie's recital.

"You have no idea who it might have been?"

"None. And I had plenty of time to think about it, believe me. That horrible dog yard is my only clue. Maybe it was the owner. I don't know. Like I said, he came up behind me, and I didn't hear anything because those mutts were making so much noise. When I woke up I was blindfolded—couldn't see a thing. Just heard the door shut as he left."

"What was it he told you again?"

"Warned me that I'd be sorry if I didn't keep the chain tight and not to take off the blindfold until he was gone."

"How did you get it off?" Jensen asked.

"It was loosely tied. All I had to do was rub my face against my arm and it fell off."

"Odd. Seems like it would have been more frightening if you couldn't see, and he was obviously trying to terrorize you."

Jessie shook her head, helpless to answer. "I think maybe he wanted me to see just how helpless I was in the trap he'd made for us. I really think he intended for both of us to die out there—Tank first. But he had no idea how well Tank trusts and minds me, did he?"

There were a few more questions, but she had told them everything she could remember.

"Now," she said when she had given the last answer, "your turn. Tell me everything that's happened since I left."

Becker sketched out the situation for her and how it had developed, but he didn't take long or go into much detail.

Jessie sat thinking hard when he had finished. "And you really think my abduction is connected to the two murders? Tell me why again—those specific points."

"Wease has to be the person who took Tank from the fairground and made threats to you over the telephone, though I don't know how we'll ever prove it. It makes sense because he claimed the camera bag—wanted it back when it was returned. He'd seen Danny Tabor with you at the Iditarod booth—chased the boy away from there, in fact. But we don't think he was the person who hit you and took you to the cabin. How could he have known where you'd be? There was too much time involved for him to have gone out there, done that, and not been missed from his security job at the fair.

Lomax seems to keep pretty careful track of his people and would have noticed. He fired Wease for not showing up on time."

"And you think Wease killed the other guy?"

"We can prove that he and Belmont—the body in the pond—were connected. More than one person saw them together, one of them Danny, who saw them that same night. Both Wease and Belmont are dead, so it was someone else who made an attempt to grab Danny yesterday morning—and that may be the same person who grabbed you. We need to know who that person is. Danny got a good look and can identify him. So we're taking him to have a look at the rest of the security staff this morning."

"Good idea. But can you please take me home first?"

Becker and Jensen gave each other questioning looks.

"How about after?" Jensen asked her, with a glance at his watch. "We're supposed to meet them at the fairground in half an hour."

"Can I come with you? Who knows, I might recognize someone."

Jensen grinned, knowing it was unlikely, but willing to humor her. "Phil?"

"Okay—okay." Becker gave in. "Let's get you checked out and you can come along. Alex can take you home and get you settled when we're through."

CHAPTER 28

"I hate hospitals," Jessie informed the living room group in reaction to Becker's comment that he'd never seen anybody leave one with more enthusiasm.

"You weren't winning any footraces with that knee, but you took first prize for exuberance."

"It also took longer getting to the security office with you along," Jensen said. "Seemed like everybody had heard you were missing and wanted you to know they were glad you were okay."

Jessie smiled, remembering.

"It's great to have friends," she said.

They parked in the employee lot at the fairground and slowly walked through to the security office. Passing between the lumberjack arena and the back of The Sluice Box, Becker pointed at the small grove of trees with the picnic table.

"That's where you saw the guy you thought was drunk that night, right? From what we know now, it *was* Belmont, and the bartender *did* throw him out the back door."

As if he had been conjured by Becker's words, Jessie's friend Eric came out the back door of the pub suddenly with a load of trash destined for the Dumpster. "Hey, Jessie. We were worried about you." Tossing the trash, he came to meet them and give her a careful hug, mindful of her obvious injuries. "You all right? What happened?"

"I'll be fine," she told him. "I'll come and fill you in later, okay? I'm already slowing these guys up for a meeting with my hobbling."

"Sure thing. It'll keep, and I'll keep a beer cold for you."

He greeted the two troopers and waved them off with a grin as he went back toward the pub.

They made it as far as the Iditarod booth before they were stopped again. This time it was Joanne Potts who came out the door in a rush to greet Jessie. "Thank God," she called while she was still in motion. "I was worried to death. Did you find Tank?"

Jessie assured her that her lead dog was safe and sound. "But I've done the damn-damns to this knee again, so I won't be able to help you."

"Not to worry. I've got all kinds of help. Barbara Brosier is back from Alabama, and two more people suddenly volunteered yesterday."

Once again Jessie promised to tell her later about what had happened, then limped on to the security office with

Becker and Jensen, where they found Danny Tabor and his father waiting for them outside.

"Hello, Danny," she said, stopping beside him. "I hear you've been having quite a time. So have I."

"Hi," Danny said with a grin that was a bit bashful but that revealed the devotion Jessie seemed to inspire in kids. "How's your dog Tank?"

"He's just fine."

"This is my dad," Danny told her, remembering his manners.

"Doug," his father said, holding out a hand, but quickly withdrawing it when he saw the condition of hers.

"Sorry," she said, "but it's good to meet you. You have a fine boy here. He's good with dogs."

"He's lobbying for one."

She turned back to Danny. "You know, I may have some new puppies soon. Maybe you should come and pick one."

A huge grin spread itself over Danny's face.

"A bit out of our price range, I think," Doug Tabor said, knowing the value of a pedigreed animal from a sled dog racing kennel.

She smiled at the boy, whose grin had disappeared in disappointment. "That, I think, might be arranged between Danny and me, if you approve. I sometimes need help with my dogs, and he needs to learn about how to take care of one. We could make a trade."

"Oh, Dad, can I?" Danny asked, starry-eyed and anxious. "Please?"

Tabor grinned and nodded to Jessie.

"That's generous of you, but we'll wait till Danny's through being grounded and see how it goes. He's promised to be more responsible."

"Really responsible," Danny said, eagerly reaffirming his promise.

Becker grinned, aware of exactly how this deal would eventually turn out—to the satisfaction of all concerned. "Let's go in," he suggested. "We need to get this done before the fair opens. These people have to go to work. You ready, Danny?"

Danny's hopeful grin quickly turned to anxiety.

"It'll be fine—and easy," Becker told him. "Remember what I told you. All you have to do is look around and tell me if you see the man who came after you in the truck. Okay? That's all. Nobody can hurt you. We'll be right there all the time."

The boy turned to Jessie. "Will you come with me?" he asked her.

"Sure," she said, encouraged by a nod from Becker. "I'll be glad to."

Reassured, he walked close beside her as they followed Becker through the door, Doug Tabor and Jensen close behind.

Inside they found a staff meeting in progress and the room crowded with people wearing black SECURITY T-shirts and baseball caps. Becker had arranged with Dave Lomax not to tell his staff that Danny would be coming to their meeting, or why, so several of those assembled turned questioning looks on the group as they all filed in.

It was crowded enough so that when Becker leaned and casually lifted Danny to a waist-high counter, it seemed that his intention was to make space, when it was really to position the boy so he could see everyone in the room. Jessie stepped up beside Danny and slipped an arm around his waist.

"Can we help you with something?" one of the security guards asked.

"Phil Becker, Alaska state troopers."

"Oh, right. Dave said you'd be coming. He'll be right back."

"That's okay. I need your attention for just a minute. I won't keep you, because I know you have to get to work when the fair opens. You all know about the murder in the lumberjack arena," he told them. "I'd like to ask your help in telling us anything suspicious that you might have seen or heard, however insignificant it might seem."

As Becker spoke, Danny cautiously examined face after face around the room. When the trooper paused to look at him, he shook his head.

"You sure?" Becker asked softly.

"Yes. I don't see him," the boy whispered.

"Okay."

He turned back to the group of security guards. "I don't need to know immediately, especially if you're supposed to be somewhere else right now. But I'll be around, or you can reach me through our office here in Palmer. Thanks for your time. We'll let you get on with it."

Lifting Danny down, Becker led the way outside, where he knelt beside the boy.

"You are absolutely sure you didn't recognize the man in the truck?" he asked again.

"I'm sure. He wasn't there."

"Well, Lomax told me that a few of them wouldn't be there—already on duty around the grounds. So that's the best we can do for now."

"Sorry," Danny said, still sticking close to Jessie.

"You don't need to be sorry," she said and gave him a hug. "You did *great!*"

While the five walked back toward the parking lot, Becker and Jensen discussed the failure in low tones, while Danny answered some of Jessie's questions about his runaway time at the fairground, making her laugh at his scarecrow deception.

"I'd like to have seen that," she told him. "Bet you made a good one."

"Mr. Monroe said I did. I stayed really still."

"Who's Mr. Monroe?"

"A nice old man who hid out with me."

They had reached The Sluice Box when Jessie remembered her promise to tell the bartender about her disappearance.

"Do we have time?" she asked Jensen. "Or do you need to get me home quickly?"

He questioned his partner with a raise of eyebrows.

Becker gave in. "I should get back to the—oh, what the hell. Let's all get something to drink. Fair's just open, but the pub won't be for another half-hour." My treat. Danny's under age, but he's with two law enforcement officers, and the place is closed and empty, so I think we can bend a rule in favor of a soft drink this one time. Okay, Doug?"

"Why not?"

They all trooped in through the back door.

The double front door was closed, which made it darker than usual inside, but the bar space was brightly lighted. Eric was nowhere to be seen. There were only two people. A man with his back to them was standing at the far end of the bar, so intent on hitting on the blond woman Becker had seen the night before that he didn't even notice them. She was continuing to set up what would be needed when the place opened and was obviously trying to ignore him.

All the picnic tables were empty, so Becker led them to the one nearest the bar.

Eric almost immediately came out of the cooler, saw them and came around to greet them with a grin. "Great. Glad you came back. Looks like you've picked up a midget along the way," he said, referring to Danny, who looked up and frowned.

"I'm not a midget," he declared indignantly.

"You must be," Eric told him. "We can't serve kids, so you have to be a midget for a little while. Okay?"

"Okay," Danny agreed, to accompanying smiles. "I'll be a midget—but only for as long as it takes to drink one root beer."

"Root beer—coming right up. What can I get for the rest of you nonmidgets?"

They ordered a mix of soft drinks and beer, Jessie choosing a Killian's Red. "I dreamed of one for two whole days. I don't care if it's too early in the morning—I'm having it."

"Be right back," Eric told them.

"I'll come and help," Becker offered, and they went to fill the order.

Everyone was quiet for a moment. The only thing to be heard was the sound of bottles being opened, beer being poured, and the woman's slightly irritated voice from the other end of the bar.

"Give it up. I told you, I've got a boyfriend."

"Oh, come on, darlin'. Your secret's safe with me," the man's voice answered.

At Jensen's side, Jessie suddenly grew rigid as she straightened in incredulity and shock.

Thinking he had accidentally bumped her injured knee, Jensen turned to apologize, only to see that all the color had drained from her distracted face and she looked ready to faint.

"Jessie?" he asked, lifting an arm to support her. *"Jessie?"*

"That's *him,*" she whispered through stiff lips. "That's the voice of the man in the cabin. I knew I'd heard it somewhere before. Who is that?"

"You sure?"

"Positive."

"Oh, hell. You're no fun. I've gotta get back to work anyway," the man at the bar said to the blond, turned, and started in their direction.

At the sight of him, Danny seemed to shrink. Sliding lower and lower on the attached bench of the table, he disappeared under it with a gasp. "That's the guy from the truck."

"Hey, Dave. I just talked to your—"

The tray of full plastic cups Becker was carrying went flying as Dave Lomax knocked it from his hands in a dash for the door.

CHAPTER 29

Lomax had purposely stayed away from the staff meeting, knowing Danny could identify him," Becker told the assembled group in Jessie's living room. "He figured that since The Sluice Box was closed, it would be a perfect place to avoid being seen."

"That would have worked, too, if we hadn't just happened to go in," Jessie added. "I was stunned to hear that voice again."

Each of those listening knew parts of Lomax's capture, but few knew it all, so a barrage of questions resulted from the disclosure of his attempt to escape.

"So he *killed Wease?"*

"Who else was involved?"

"What about the man with the rainbow hair?"

"Who killed the man in the pond?"

The sound woke Danny, who sat up blinking sleepily at the confusion of voices. Tank rolled over to sit up beside him.

Becker threw up his hands defensively. "Whoa! Let us tell you the rest—then we'll answer questions, okay? Alex, you helped get him, so you go first."

Jensen puffed thoughtfully at his pipe and smiled. "Eric was the one who brought him down," he said. "Set what he was carrying on the bar without spilling a drop of Danny's root beer and tackled Lomax in a flying leap that flattened him on the sawdust floor. But he put up a struggle, so I helped. Then we arrested him and took him in for questioning."

"Which he refused to have any part of," Becker interjected. "Lawyered up immediately."

"So how did you formulate conclusions concerning his culpability?" Frank Monroe asked quietly.

"Well, for a start, you identified his truck. There is evidence that I can't talk about now but that will come out at his trial. But I can tell you that it's admissible and he's charged with kidnapping, murder, and conspiracy to commit robbery. Once Jessie and Danny had officially identified him, we knew what to look for, and where. Some of it took lab work, right, John?" he said to Timmons.

Timmons agreed with a nod. "We're still at it, but we've verified a lot. There was one significant fingerprint in Wease's kitchen, for instance."

"You arrested another man, didn't you?" asked Doug Tabor.

"The owner of the dog yard where Jessie was hit. He's evidently a buddy of Lomax's who was in on the plan. We think they intended to hide the money in his yard once it was stolen. Then Lomax could have played innocent and helped with the investigation that followed. We searched that yard—a nasty job if ever I had one—and found some yellow cord that matched what they

used around Tank's neck in that old cabin where they stashed him—and Jessie. They both had a hand in that—using the four-wheeler and moving your truck, Jess. Where you left it was too close to the dog yard. But it was *Lomax who whispered to you in that cabin."*

"But why would he need me? Did he plan it all along—and if so, why?"

"We don't think so. I think it was having you show up at that dog yard that did it—an opportunity he couldn't afford to miss. He tied you and Tank up with whatever was handy. The chain and rope both came from that yard, which was a poor choice and indicates no prior planning. Also, it happened after Wease killed Belmont, so Lomax may have figured you'd be good insurance in case Wease was caught and implicated his cohorts to save his hide. Lomax probably killed Wease for the same reason—so he couldn't talk."

Jessie nodded. "So I was just in the wrong place at the wrong time?"

"I think so, but he's not talking, so it's speculation. His dog-yard buddy, on the other hand, is scared enough to make a deal, so I'll let you know."

"But couldn't Lomax have killed both Wease and Belmont?"

Becker took up the story as Jensen paused to light the pipe that had gone out as he talked. "We think Wease killed Belmont. They obviously had some kind of disagreement. Maybe Belmont wanted out. But there's no evidence to connect Lomax with that one."

"What about the man with the rainbow hair?" Danny spoke up. "I saw him talking to the man who chased me first."

Becker smiled. "Actually, he had nothing to do with any of it," he assured the boy. "Just talking to a bad guy doesn't make him one, too. He told us Wease just asked him if he had seen you."

"Good. I liked his hair."

"Oh, dear," his mother said, casting a mock long-suffering look at the ceiling. "Here we go again."

"I think it's time we took this young man home and put him to bed," her husband said, sliding forward on the sofa. "He needs to make an early start on those chores tomorrow."

"Aw," said Danny, but he smiled as he threw an arm around Tank to give him a hug good-bye.

Tank licked his ear affectionately in return, making Jessie smile as well.

As the rest of the company began to rise and agree that it was getting late, Monroe asked Jensen a final question. "Did Ron Wease steal the dog from the Iditarod booth?"

"We think it had to be Wease. That may also be part of why Lomax killed him. Wease probably panicked, knowing what might be figured out from the pictures if they were developed, and hoped he could scare Jessie into getting them back from Danny. When you were hiding under the table, you heard him tell someone on the phone—probably Lomax—that he'd take care of some problem with 'Curt.' If he killed *Belmont to take care of that problem, whatever it was, Lomax may have decided that he was too large a threat—that he was doing things on his own personal agenda and could blow the whole plan."*

Monroe rose from his comfortable chair, dropped his pipe into a pocket, and stepped to offer a hand to Jensen. "It's been good to meet you," he said quietly. "Take care of our girl."

"I'll try, if she'll let me."

"Oh, I have high hopes for that." And with a conspiratorial twinkle in the glance he tossed in her direction, Monroe strolled off to collect his hat and cane.

Slowly those who had gathered to share their perspectives on the preceding few days said their good-byes and departed in their waiting vehicles. Frank Monroe rode with the Tabors, who had practically adopted him—though it might have been the other way around. Jensen and Becker carried John Timmons, wheelchair and all, down the front steps, then found further assistance unnecessary as he skillfully settled himself for the drive back to Anchorage in his specially equipped station wagon. They climbed back up to where Jessie and Tank stood waiting on the porch and waved him off.

"I'm off, too," Becker said. "It's good to know you're home safe, Jessie. And your new house is great—much better than the one that burned."

"I think so, too," she told him. "Thanks, Phil, for everything. What would I do without you?"

She gave him a hug and he started down the steps again. "You'd do fine," he tossed back over a shoulder. "You've got Jensen to keep you from straying into harm's way."

"As if!"

"Oh, yes." His voice came back from where he had parked his truck. "I doubt we've seen the last of your independent adventures."

Before she could answer, they heard the sound of the truck door closing.

Jensen chuckled. "You can't always have the last word, Jess.

He's getting wise to you. Come on, I'll help you clean up the remains of the party."

Half an hour later the job was done, Tank had been returned to his place in the dog yard, and they had settled on the sofa with cups of tea. The fire crackled cheerfully in the cast-iron stove, and the dragon-shaped humidifier atop it puffed steam into the room through its nostrils.

"Do you have all the answers now, Jess?" Alex asked. "Anything you still have questions about?"

She was silent for a moment, staring into what she could see of the flames, then turned to face him. "Only one," she said. "Why did you come back?"

It was his turn to gather thoughts before answering. "Not just because you were missing," he said finally. "That was part of my coming back so quickly, but I was on my way already—had already talked to Commander Swift and hired back on. I came because everything I want is here, and"—a smile hovered on his lips—"because my mother told me to."

"Your mother?"

"Yes. She told me—with some exasperation—that I'd better go north because I was just existing in Idaho and doing myself no good."

"Sounds like her. Do you always do what she tells you, then?"

"Only when she's right. And I knew she was."

He hesitated, then went on. "It's really very simple, Jess. I missed you. I love you. Do you still love me?"

"You know I do. You don't just stop loving someone when they're not around. But we're different people now."

"Are we?"

"Yes. We'll have to figure everything out again."

"Will we?"

There was a long pause as they said things to each other without words.

"No," Jessie said at length. "We won't. They're just details that will figure us out, won't they?"

Then, for a time, there were no more questions—just answers.

"I noticed," Alex said, holding her close and feeling more himself than he had in a long time, "that you have a new brass bed and managed somehow to rescue your favorite northern lights quilt from the fire."

"Hm-m-m," said Jessie in his ear. "You noticed that, did you?"

ACKNOWLEDGMENTS

With sincere thanks to:

Everyone who works hard, year-round and during its end-of-summer run, to make the annual Alaska State Fair happen smoothly and well in Palmer—especially to Pam Troutman for answering many questions.

The security staff and EMTs who were generous with information and ideas.

The staff of The Sluice Box pub for information, good humor, and beer.

The lumberjacks for a great show.

Becky Lundqvist for sharing her medical expertise and for editorial assistance.

My son Eric of Art Forge Unlimited for designing the maps.

My talented editor, Sarah Durand.

My dependable agent, Dominick Abel.

Travel with female musher Jessie Arnold,
in Sue Henry's ALASKA MYSTERY series

As if the bone-chilling and dangerous world of dog-sledding isn't risky enough, accomplished musher Jessie Arnold always seems to find extra trouble on and off the trail. Whether it's the dead body of a fellow musher, a runaway accused of murder, or the kidnapping of a young friend, without fail, intrigue tracks Jessie across the frozen tundra of the Alaskan wilderness.

Enjoy the pages to follow, which give a glimpse into the world of Jessie and her State Trooper love interest, Alex Jensen.

The winner of Alaska's world-famous Iditarod—a grueling, eleven-hundred-mile dog-sled race across a frigid Arctic wilderness—takes home a $25,000 purse. But in **Murder on the Iditarod Trail**, *the prize is survival. With the top contenders dying one by one, Jessie Arnold, Alaska's premier female "musher," fears she may be the next victim.*

She was, as Bomber had put it, pretty broke up. One side of her face was badly scraped, and her body felt strangely flexible as they lifted her out of the snow and onto the sleeping bag they found in her sled. Although her shoulders were muscular beneath the heavy parka, Hensen thought she looked too small and fragile to be an Iditarod racer. Her knitted cap had come off, and her hair, braided into one long plait, had pulled out in childish wisps that curled slightly around her ears. He tucked the hat into her parka pocket, where he found a penlight, a half-eaten Snickers bar, extra clips for the harness, and several hair-pins. Zipped into the opposite pocket were a coin purse with a few dollars, her driver's and fishing licenses, and school pictures of two little boys, aged perhaps six and eight.

As they wrestled the broken sled out toward the trail, the thump of rotors suddenly extinguished the silence. They looked up to see Becker waving from the passenger seat. He had been out to the site of the helicopter. Slowly, conscious of the narrow sides of the gorge, Lehrman allowed the machine to settle into a section of the trail flat enough to accommodate the landing. Carefully he tested the stability of the snow before committing to more than a hover. Finding it solid enough support, he set down, but only eased off on the power.

With little time to go through the contents of the sled bag, Alex made a cursory search for anything unusual. He fashioned a cradle from strong line to support the sled so the helicopter could lift it from the gorge. Stepping around, he examined the section of gang line still attached. It was too even to break. It had been cut most of the way through with something very sharp; only a small part of the rope was frayed from the tension that had pulled it apart. He taped an evidence bag over this end and marked it for attention in the lab. It didn't make sense for Ginny to have cut her own line, but an accident of some kind couldn't be ruled out completely. If, as he suspected, the line had been cut by someone else, it couldn't have guaranteed her death. Whoever cut it had not cared when or where it would break—they just hoped for a serious accident. With the added strain of the sharp turns in the gorge, chances had been good it would happen there. It could have put her out of the race whatever the result.

Rugged outdoorsman Jack Hampton's vacation takes a turn for the worse when he discovers a prospector's diary from the 1800s. It seems that the diary has brought him all kinds of bad luck, including a false rap that he's killed a controversial ex-Senator. But State Trooper Alex Jensen isn't convinced of Hampton's guilt, and in **Termination Dust**, *he must track the bitter truth through the treacherous snows of the Yukon Wilderness.*

A journal. Hampton could scarcely believe he had found the journal of a participant of the Klondike gold rush, but it could be nothing else. A very real man had recorded his small part of the incredible rush for gold in the Yukon almost a hundred years ago. He turned a page to see what Riser had written. It began with a date and a place: Sunday, September 5, Steamship *Al-ki*, Headed for Alaska Territory.

The writing was neat and not difficult to decipher, but small, two lines in each ruled section of the page, an indication that the writer had been concerned with conserving his supply of paper. Hampton turned some of the other pages delicately and the penmanship remained the same throughout, crowding as much onto each page as possible. At the back, half a dozen pages had not been filled and after them two or three leaves had been torn out, leaving ragged remnants where they had been.

Turning back to the first entry, Hampton frowned, considering his find. If he had gone to Dawson, how had Riser's journal found its way here, almost twenty miles beyond that community? Laying down the journal, he picked up the boot. Not only his journal, but Riser himself had apparently reached this location.

Carefully he emptied the bones into his hand. The individual yellowed pieces were so clean they seemed almost artificial, pleasing in their shape and smoothness to his fingers, divorced and distanced from their original function and purpose. It was possible to see how a few of them fit together as easily as they had in life, even without the tendons and flesh that had held them together and made them move. Though nature had picked them clean, some of the vanished tethers had worn reminders of their presence into the very bone itself, leaving evidence of their flexing, if one looked closely.

Pilot Norm Lewis hasn't been seen since his plane went down six months ago over the vast white wilderness. And when an unidentified woman is found strapped to the passenger seat of his downed Cessna, Lewis's wife, Rochelle, joins State Trooper Alex Jensen, as they try to find a man who vanished without a trace—leaving behind only a bundle of troublesome secrets. **Sleeping Lady** *will have you trekking through the wilderness with Alex and Rochelle as they try to unravel the pilot's disappearing act.*

The four walked single file, Caswell bringing up the rear, over the top and down the other side, where part of the tail of a plane could be seen above a screen of brush on the lakeshore. Landreth slipped, slid, and swore a couple of times, but made it. In a few minutes they were gathered next to a bettered fuselage, the nose of which was still partly sunk in mud and water beyond the bank. A winch attached to an outcropping of rock had been employed to drag the wreck almost free of the lake, and its weathered and dirty condition, except for the top of the vertical tail and rudder, very much evidenced its season underwater. The registration number, however, could easily be read through the grime. It was definitely the aircraft in which Lewis had disappeared.

Water still ran an slowly from under it, tracing small channels in the mud on both sides as it made its way downhill and back into the lake. Both doors were closed, and though the window was partially opaque with sediment from the water, a human shape could be seen inside. The broken fuselage smelled wet and dank, and underlying that was a cloying hint of something else that was grossly unpleasant.

"Don't touch anything," Jensen cautioned.

"They've scrambled the lab boys out of Anchorage and they'll be here soon to get what they can, but it won't be much.

Chelle nodded, numbly, her eyes wide, but it soon became obvious that her mind was anything but numb. After a minute she moved without speaking, walked slowly around the plane, pausing twice—once to look up the slope where the tops of three or four narrow spruce were broken off in a direct line with the ruined fuselage, and once when she reached the door on the left side.

Jensen stepped up beside her, pointing.

"Bullet hole," he said.

Without actually touching it, he drew a circle with one finger around a puncture in the metal below the window on the passenger side. The way the metal was creased, angling slightly, gave the impression it had been shot from below.

"Another. There." He pointed to a similar hole in the engine cowling. "This wasn't an accident. Someone shot this plane out of the air."

Jessie Arnold and her beau, Alex Jensen, are excited to be participating in a unique trip—a re-creation of the famous 1897 Alaskan Inside Passage voyage. But the strange disappearance—and probable death—of a crew member brings a halt to all the fun. Now Alex must once again use his State Trooper training to save the rest of the passengers and crew, as **Death Takes Passage.**

A pounding on the door interrupted what he had been about to say.

Don Sawyer stood outside, a stricken expression on his face.

"You'd better come, Jensen," he said in a strained, flat-sounding voice. "One of the passengers just spotted a . . . a . . ."

"What, Don? What?"

" . . . b-body."

"What?"

" . . . a bo . . ." he couldn't say it again.

"A body? Where?"

"In the . . . water." He was practically hyperventilating.

Jessie grabbed his arm and pulled and shoved him to a seat on Alex's bed. "Put your head between your knees," she told him over her shoulder, heading to the bathroom for a glass of water.

Alex suddenly realized that as they talked the *Spirit* had come to a complete stop. He grabbed his jacket and promptly left Jessie to take care of Sawyer.

In **Deadfall**, *Iditarod musher Jessie Arnold is being stalked and terrorized by an anonymous enemy. First one of her sled dogs is badly injured by a steel trap intentionally set for that purpose, and then threatening phone calls and unsigned messages follow. But in a plan gone horribly wrong, Jessie ends up alone on a secluded island, with only the madman to keep her company.*

The husky pulled her forward until they reached the outer edge of the wide lot, the last row of boxes, close to a hundred yards from the cabin. A few feet from one box in particular, he halted, stared at it, and growled deep in his throat. Hackles rose along his neck and back, bristling under her hand. Her light showed nothing but the wooden side of it.

"Alex?"

He stepped up beside her, the shotgun ready for instant use, should he need it.

Then Jessie could hear it again, a muffled whining that came repeatedly, and the familiar wet sound of a dog licking something, but the sharp crack that had broken her sleep did not come the second time. She shone the light over the outside of the dog box. Alex's light moved over the dirt that surrounded it, stopped, and returned to the ground close to the door.

Jessie caught her breath.

It was soaked with red—blotches of blood that continued into the box.

"God. What the hell?"

They stepped forward and leaned to peer cautiously in through the door. Her light found the dog that had struggled to crawl inside and lay on the straw facing them. The straw under it was also liberally stained with scarlet. The dog raised its head to look blindly into the flashlight beam, quivered, then resumed licking, but it had been enough for them to see the ugly metal trap that was clamped cruelly to the flesh of one foreleg.

Musher Jessie Arnold encounters a new challenge at every turn of the icy trail. This time, a young fellow musher is abducted, and when the kidnappers call to inform Jessie, they warn her to keep the information a secret, or else the girl will die. So as she struggles along the toughest sled race in the world, she must also do her best to prevent a **Murder on the Yukon Quest.**

For several nights a moose had wandered close to the cabin, exciting the dogs and provoking them to vocalize loudly at what their tethers prevented them from chasing. Jessie had grinned to herself at the tracks she found in the snow, for the huge ungulate seemed to exhibit a sense of humor in coming exactly close enough to cause a ruckus without actually challenging so many canines. Its passing had left large divided hoofprints at the bottom of holes in the deep snow as it moved around the circumference of the yard on long gangly legs, munching on the willows that grew by the drive, even lying down to rest in a stand of birch and spruce to the north, pointedly ignoring the protests of the restless dogs.

Now, as she heard them barking again, Jessie smiled drowsily, rolled onto her left side, and drifted back to sleep in the middle of the big brass bed she usually shared with Alex. There would undoubtedly be more tracks to be found in the morning, but they were really nothing to worry about. A bear might have been different, for some bears will kill and eat dogs, especially those that could not escape. But, thankfully, all the bears, plump from a long summer banquet, were elsewhere, tucked up securely into their dens, keeping warm in their heavy fur, contentedly slumbering the winter away.

Though the dogs barked once or twice after that, Jessie did not wake again. She was unaware that, after the cabin had been dark for over an hour, a dark figure has slipped stealthily into the dog yard from between two large spruce trees; that he had watched Jessie come home from her training run, care for her dogs, and go inside. Walking slowly between the straw-filled boxes, he picked one, knelt, and silenced the dog by petting its head, rubbing its ears, and speaking in a low voice.

When he stood up and moved on to another, the first dog followed to where its tethers should have stopped it, but found that it was unexpectedly free of restraint. It stopped, not used to being without impediment, then moved on, pursuing the man. When it found a running mate was also on the loose, the two decided it was time to play, and enthusiastically accompanied the provider of their liberty as he quietly made his way out of the yard and down the long driveway to Knik Road. Reaching the truck he had parked a bend or two away, they willingly jumped up into the cab at his invitation and rode away with him into the night.

In **Beneath the Ashes**, *Jessie Arnold must determine whether there may be more to her desperate friend than meets the eye. The suspicious blaze that leveled her favorite local pub disrupts Jessie's off-season dogsled training. And when she starts to look more closely at her friend's strange behavior, she must decide whether the woman is a terrified victim, or a killer.*

It was growing colder. The sun had followed them over the last hill and now shone on the west side. Though it shed very little warmth this time of year, even the illusion of it disappeared on the east side that they now travelled. The frosty blue-purple shade was darker in the shadows of the few sparse trees. It would be good to reach their goal and get a fire built in the stove to warm the cabin in which they would spend the night. Anne wiggled restlessly on the sled, looking ahead eagerly at each corner of the hillside, headed southwest on the east-facing hill.

They came at last to a sharp bend that Jessie remembered, knowing that, as soon as they rounded it, she would be able to see the Holman cabin ahead through the trees.

They turned, but she could see nothing but trees—

dead trees, black and scorched. The cabin was gone.

"Oh, Anne, it's burned down," she said in surprised regret.

Halting the dogs, she stood staring at the spot where the cabin had been, then glanced down at the face of her friend, expecting to find similar consternation there.

What she saw was anything but. Anne was slowly nodding and smiling.

"Yes," she said, "I knew it was. Greg burned it—when we left."

As she tries to escape her dark past once again, Jessie Arnold temporarily puts her dogsled to rest and borrows a friend's motor home. But as she heads **Dead North**, *Jessie invites trouble when she picks up a teenage hitchhiker. She soon finds out that the boy is wanted in connection with a deadly double-murder, and if she doesn't act fast, her seemingly compassionate act may get her killed.*

A loose dog might have helped itself to the sandwich, even the cookies, in her absence, but no dog would have—could have—so quickly gulped them down and taken the apple too. A child? One of the teenage boys? Jessie quickly turned to examine the area nearby, but no questionable person was to be seen. The boys were gone, and all the family members were seated at the table—even Michael, who, unwilling to lose his ice cream treat, was now rapidly scooping potato salad from a paper plate with a plastic spoon. Who then? Someone had obviously stolen the rest of her lunch. The more she thought about it, the more annoyed Jessie became. Who the hell would have the nerve to take someone else's food?

The crunch of steps on gravel made her spin around frowning at an elderly couple who were walking past the Winnebago. They widened their eyes a little at her startled movement and accusing stare but did not stop moving in the direction of the Fort Steele entrance and gift shop.

"Hello," the white-haired man said and nodded. "Nice dog."

Flustered at her suspicious reaction, Jessie forced herself to relax and smile a little. "Ah—thanks."

The woman looked back once over her shoulder and murmured something to her husband that Jessie couldn't hear. He shrugged and they trudged steadily away in their matching blue windbreakers and white Adidas.

Feeling embarrassed and a little silly as she watched them go, Jessie suddenly noticed a figure moving toward the gift shop ahead of them at a faster than normal pace. From across the wide lot, she couldn't tell if the person was a male or female, but it was dressed in jeans, hiking boots, and a green plaid shirt. A blue backpack with a sleeping bag tied under it bounced a bit on the person's shoulders, and a denim hat with a floppy brim covered the hair. From Jessie's point of view, the person, man or woman, looked younger than herself but larger and older than the boys that had passed earlier—how old was impossible to tell. As she watched, the figure turned slightly to glance back and she could see that the face was hidden behind a large pair of sunglasses. Noticing the focus of Jessie's attention, the person immediately broke into a trot and vanished through the door to the gift shop.

Just when Jessie Arnold thinks she's put her dark past behind her, and she can safely concentrate on her dog-sledding career, excavation on her new cabin unearths a decades-old skeleton. In **Cold Company**, *a brutal slayer who has been in hiding for twenty years reemerges to find some fresh victims. And the clues that Jessie is uncovering hint that she may be the next on his list.*

Walking around the hole, Jessie went down the ramp that Peterson had scraped out as access for his Bobcat. As she moved out of the sunlight into shadow, the scent of the recently disturbed earth rose up sweetly to meet her, and she was reminded of her plans to use some of this rich soil on her vegetable garden. She crossed the flat bottom of the pit, some of the damp loam sticking to her boots, and stopped to examine the object that had caught her eye.

It lay a little less than halfway down the wall, perhaps four feet from the upper edge and six from the bottom of the pit. The small amount of what was exposed seemed smoother and of a different texture than the stone she anticipated. She frowned and started to reach up for it but then hesitated, a hint of puzzled recognition slowly dawning.

Carefully, with one gloved hand, she was brushing at the dirt that clung to the object when, without warning, a large clod suddenly came loose from one side and fell to the ground at her feet. Jessie reacted with a gasp, clenched her fingers into a fist, and pulled them back hard against her chest as she took a step away and gaped in disbelief at what hung still half buried in the wall before her. The falling soil had revealed that the complete shape was not symmetrically curved as expected. Half turned in her direction, a round dirt-packed eye socket seemed to stare blindly over her head at the now-fading light of the setting sun, and a jawbone full of teeth appeared to grin in ironic if silent approval of its unexpected liberation. It was an old skull, nothing left but bone, pale and long abandoned by its owner, but unmistakably—alarmingly—human.